Infernal

Eighteen

About the Author:
The proud son of two 20-year Navy veterans, Don A. Martinez holds a Bachelor of Arts degree in writing, and a Master of Arts degree in English with a focus on myth and folklore, both from Buffalo State College (New York). He works as a college writing professor in Texas, where he lives with his wife, daughter, and four cats.

Other Books by Don A. Martinez:
The Phantom Squadron Series
The Advance Guard
Dinétah Dragon
The Insurgent's Journal

Infernal Eighteen

Don A. Martinez

Desert Coyote Productions
Longview, Texas

**The author wishes to offer sincere thanks to author David Bruce. *Dante's
Inferno: A Retelling in Prose* is available in e-book format for free from
Smashwords and all fine e-book retailers.**

Library of Congress Control Number: 2012949115.
EAN-13: 978-0-9859379-0-4
ISBN-10: 0-9859379-0-4

Typeset in 11pt Times New Roman
Printed in the U.S.A.
First edition 2013

For Stacey and Kahlan, my reasons for existence.

Contents

Where to bad folks go when they die?
They don't go to Heaven where the angels fly
They go to the lake of fire and fry
Won't see 'em again 'til the Fourth of July
—Nirvana

Transcriber's Foreword

The last entry in the second of Alanna Sharpe's journals, dated July 2028, jolted me. Not only because of the shock of the events, but also the simple betrayal I felt right alongside her.

Cole Sharpe was a family friend. I worried about him the whole time I interviewed his wife Ariel, wondered why he had not shown up at all. To my relief, he appeared on the last night I spent in the Sharpe house, and we spent a lot of time discussing his perspective on some of Ariel's story. There's no way he could have betrayed her like this, betrayed his daughter. Even though she was only three when I talked to Ariel, the love that I felt between Cole and Alanna was …

Well, "beautiful" is the word that came to mind before. Something like "tragic" came now. I could not believe it was the truth, even though it was outlined right there for me, in Alanna's own hand:

> *The crack continues to form, until it's completely across the eye shields, completely crossing his face. They shatter, almost in slow motion. They fall off of the man's face.*
> *It's one I know very well.*
> *It's my father.*

Up to this point, she was assuming that Tyrelius Scolar, the Chairman of the Joint Chiefs of Staff for the New Empire of America, had simply been another commander she would have to destroy. She held a great deal of anger toward him, toward the Regent administration which rules the nation with an iron fist, and to the entire Supernatural Suppression Agency. With every passing word, she transferred that anger to me.

Now I was sharing her betrayal, as well.

The remainder of that particular journal was completely blank. Apparently Alanna was so incensed by the turn of events that she simply stopped writing them for a while. I decided that I needed a break before I started looking for the next volume. Fortunately enough, I had lost barely any time transcribing ... the spell on the books was effective, that's for sure ... so it was still mid-morning by the time I took off the special reading glasses and stepped outside to take a walk.

A newspaper lay on the porch of my building, seemingly left there for me since I don't subscribe. What caught my eye about it, though, was the headline.

MASS NEW EMPIRE PRISONER AMNESTY

My hopeless, betrayed mood instantly lightened. Perhaps this would be it, my family would be released this time? I eagerly read the story, and although it mentioned no names, one thing stood out to me: a promise to the Canadian government that all political prisoners held within the nation's facilities would be released and permitted to return to their lives.

For many of them, that won't do a lot of good since they've spent so much time imprisoned. *But for my family, perhaps ...?*

At that moment I forgot that I wanted to take a walk. I turned and ran back up to my apartment, propping the newspaper next to my computer. The box with the journals would serve a good purpose as an easel, so that I could remind myself that this nightmare was almost over.

The journals ...

I pulled out all six of the books from the box. The weird Celtic runic symbols met my eyes, confusing them, obscuring their actual content. Two of them, at least, I knew I didn't need now, and I knew them by the colors of their covers: the two black books were the first two volumes. I set them aside, and then returned the reading glasses to my face.

Instantly time slowed down once more. I was at my leisure to read the journals, and decipher which one was the next one. As I spread the remaining books in front of me, I noticed that someone, in a different handwriting, had written a helpful set of numbers on the covers to show the sequence. I looked for number three, only to be surprised by the markings of many of the books.

Eventually I found book three, dated January-June 2029, so apparently Alanna did no journaling for nearly six months. Hopefully this would be explained in detail. I turned my attention toward getting the other books ordered, and only then noticed the weirdness of the dates:

> Book four, 18 days
> Book five, July-September 2031
> Book six, October 2031-February 2032

Now I was thoroughly confused. If the fourth book only covered 18 days, why did the fifth book not pick up until *two years* after the third one? I had assumed that each book was supposed to cover, at most, six months: what became of the missing year and a half? This was truly worth investigating, and I sincerely hoped the answers had been entered into the journals.

Working from that assumption, I cracked open the third of the journals, fired up my computer once more, and began typing what I read, a shocking continuation of Alanna's story which took her, literally, to Hell and back.

Don A. Martinez
August 2032

Infernal

Eighteen

Heart and Mind

Chapter One: Alamo

January 18th, 2029

Dad told me once the story of the people who perished at the Alamo. He called them freedom fighters, defending their independence from Mexico. He called them heroes, too: heroes who sacrificed themselves so that the republic of Texas would be free. Granted, later Texas joined the United States, became its largest oil producer, prospered under the U.S. government, but at the same time the place always kept its sense of independence. I suppose that's why they seceded again, shortly after the New Empire took power.

I stand before the Alamo now, looking up at the building's stone face, up toward the top of the arch over the doorway where a bell hangs. At this moment, I feel like those freedom fighters nearly two hundred years before.

Outnumbered, outgunned, and hopeless.

I have no apprehensions about being out in public in broad daylight like this. Not here in San Antonio, one of five capitals of the Independent Republic of Texas. I know no SSA blueshirts will come for me here, not unless they want to trigger a war. I know that I'm out of their reach. Texas is not typically thought of as a supernatural haven … most people think Canada for that sort of thing … but there's a few of us here, many of whom fled here shortly after the SSA's purges began, knowing that the people of Texas would welcome us.

I've been here now for three months. It took a lot of effort to get here, a lot of strategizing, a lot of practice flights. I wasn't quite sure whether it would be safe or not, but after what I witnessed in Traverse City, I wasn't sure of anything anymore. I'm still not quite sure.

Yet here I stand, waiting. Waiting for a reminder of that dark time, who finally taps me on the shoulder to interrupt my reverie.

"Alanna?"

I jump and unfurl my wings. I've been doing that a lot lately … perhaps out of comfort, since I know no one will turn me in if I do. I circle around, ready for a fight, only to see the worried face of Gabe Francis, holding up his hands to show he's not armed.

"Hold on, Alanna, I'm just here to talk. That's the only reason I wanted to meet you."

I feel a growl coming on. "Sure it is."

"Really. I just want to talk to you, to try to understand what's happening."

I want to explode at this man, but I know that something like that will wear my welcome quite thin with the Texans. I know I need to hold it in. I look around and spot a coffee bar nearby.

"Over there. We'll talk over a latte."

Maybe something in me wants to give a peace offering … since Gabe is constantly guzzling coffee, perhaps this will help the conversation go smoother. He nods in agreement, and we cross the street and go into the coffee shop. Once both of us have cups, we go to a nearby table and sip in silence for a few minutes, savoring the flavor of the hot beverages.

Gabe is the one who finally speaks. "How long have you been here?"

I suppose it can't hurt to tell him. "Since October or around that time. I've been living out of a backpack pretty much for the last three months, doing odd jobs, helping others out. There's a burgeoning supernatural community here, who's really helpful when you need it."

Gabe nods. "I see. What kinds of odd jobs?"

"The usual, helping with cooking, babysitting, transportation …"

"You've been flying?"

I smirk. "How did you think I got here? I threaded a needle right through the middle of the New Empire to get here from Montreal, entirely airborne. When I got here I slept for two days straight before I had my strength back."

He nods again, and then grows quiet. The only sounds we hear are the sounds of the coffee shop staff, busily attending to their customers. Finally, he looks up and softly breaks the silence. "Alanna, please tell me what's on your mind."

I sigh. It's hard to be angry for so long and yet I've wanted to be … "I think you probably know already. Why couldn't you tell me that I was trying to kill Dad?"

Gabe rubs a temple gently. "I had my instructions, Alanna. I knew that Cole was Scolar. I knew that he was the Invader."

"And yet you left that little tidbit a secret …"

"Could I please explain?" Gabe's shortness catches me quickly, and I nod. "Thank you. When we started out on this adventure last year, your explicitly stated goal was to find your parents. This was after you witnessed your mother's capture. The thing is, the disappearances of your parents are a symptom of an even greater evil, one which required a Guardsman.

"Since the Guardsman was not available, it fell to the next generation to take the Sword. Thus, now you have it."

I know for sure about that. I feel its weight against my hip every day. It doesn't leave my side at all … I almost feel like it's a fifth limb by now.

"Do you remember the night I brought you to the Ranch?"

I nod quietly. I wish I didn't.

"You were so exhausted after we got there that you passed out in my arms on the way to the house. Kitty immediately put you to bed, and I had a chance to talk with Cyrus while she was attending to you."

Please, Gabe, don't tell me Aunt Kitty and Uncle Cyrus knew all this time, too.

"I discussed the situation with Cyrus, and later Kitty when she was finished with you. I told them what I could, which did *not* include Scolar's true identity."

That's a relief.

"I told them that you would, by necessity, become an icon to the supernaturals that came to the Ranch. At this point Cyrus was halfway through with his doorway, and was preparing the house for the parade of people who would eventually be marching through it, looking for an escape."

I run my finger along the rim of my coffee cup. "An icon? What do you mean by that?"

Gabe nodded. "You are a perfect symbol for everything that's wrong with the New Empire. Your parents were taken from you at fifteen, and you were left to fend for yourself. You're persecuted and pursued by the New Empire not for anything you've done but for *who you are,* the same as any supernatural who would come through that door."

I don't feel like correcting him, telling him that now there's a reason they pursue me, because I took out Chicago single-handed. He knows this. Right now, I feel my eyes getting hot. I don't like where this is going. "Then what makes me the icon? Why does it have to be *me?*"

Gabe takes a long swallow of his latte before answering. "Because you're the Guardsman, Alanna. You're the symbol. You're the one to rally around, the one to lead the supernaturals into battle. If it weren't you, it would've been your father."

I'm not quite following here. My face shows my confusion, apparently, as Gabe continues.

"The Guardsman, traditionally, has been used as a symbol of righteousness, and especially in his earlier years prior to the 20th Century. Any side with a Guardsman has generally been thought to be blessed by God, the fated victor. So long as the supernaturals have a Guardsman on their side, they have hope."

I lean back in my chair as this sinks in. They want me to be some symbol, some great hope? Who am I really, other than a scared sixteen-year-old girl with a big Sword who, oh by the way, just *happens* to be able to fly, breathe fire, and turn into a dragon? Does that make me special, as opposed to any other supernatural? No. Does that make me someone who I'm not? Of course not.

Yet here's Gabe, sitting there patiently snorting down coffee, telling me that I'm supposed to be the rallying point of an entire rebellion.

"You still haven't really answered my first question, Gabe. Why couldn't you tell me Scolar was Dad?"

Gabe gets a sad expression on his face. "I am truly sorry, Alanna, but I was told not to. My Employer made it crystal clear to me that it was information you would need to find out for yourself, not be told. So I had to keep my mouth shut."

A memory flashes in my mind, and my eyes widen. "At Trinity Site … you knew this when we were there, when we were fighting … when you yanked me out before I could kill the Invader."

Now the tears fall. *He knew. He stopped me from killing Dad. He saved Dad from me.*

Gabe slowly nods and places a hand on my shoulder. "Alanna, we need you now. We need you back at the Ranch, we need you back out there fighting. The supernaturals need their symbol back."

His eyes rotate down, meaningfully, toward the Sword. I follow them with my hand, gripping the hilt of the weapon. "They need the Guardsman."

Gabe nods. "Will you come back to us? William misses you dearly."

I've missed him too. William White Bear, my wendigo friend … *maybe more …*

"Michika spends every day trying to get Fahaian to help her contact you."

Damn it, why does he have to start listing off my friends now? What's left of my resolve is starting to crumble, but there's still one thing I need to know.

"Can you be up front with me about one thing, Gabe?"

He shrugs. "I'll try."

My damp eyes narrow. "Can you promise me, on your Employer's Honor, that there are no more secrets you're holding back from me? Is Dad's whereabouts the only one, or am I going to learn other things as well?"

Gabe sighs and twiddles his coffee cup in his fingers. "Alanna I'm sorry, but I can't promise you that. I can be up front about one thing, though … any secrets that I do know are ones that I am under orders from my Employer to keep from you, because you are intended to discover them for yourself."

For once, I see the emotion in the agent's eyes. It's one I'm not sure I've ever seen in them before.

Regret.

I sigh. "Well, I guess that's the best you can do." I reach across the table and take his hand. "Okay, you win. I'm coming back with you. When can we leave?"

Gabe smirks and reaches into his coat. I recognize what he's pulling out, it's that same pen he had a year ago, when he sent us to the Ranch the first time.

"Whenever you're ready. They're waiting for us, I'm sure."

We both stand up and leave the coffee shop. Once we're in the middle of the street, he holds the pen above his head. I have to say something before he clicks it, so I gently tap his chest.

"Thank you, Gabe."

He looks confused. "For what? All I did was anger you."

I can't help but smile. "Yes, you did … but you also guided me the right way, and in your way you are trying to help me. So thank you … thank you for saving Dad from me. Thank you for telling me what you did today." I lean into him, awaiting the trip. "Thank you for finding me."

This time the smile Gabe gives me isn't a smirk … it's an honest-to-God smile. "You're quite welcome, Alanna. Hang on." He wraps his free arm around my shoulders and clicks the pen.

In an instant, we're back in the frigid cold of a wintry Wyoming field, though I don't know where the Hidden-In-Plain-Sight Ranch really is this time. The last time I had seen the Ranch, it was perched in the middle of the Canadian Rockies. Wherever we are, though, it's freezing cold, and I'm more prepared for mild Texas weather than a blizzard.

"Gabe, where are we?" My words are carried off with the wind, so I don't know if he heard me until he answers.

"Cyrus has been moving the Ranch on a regular basis, to try to stay ahead of the SSA. Right now he has it parked on the southern border of the Yukon."

I narrow my eyes against the blizzard, trying to see through the driving snow. I can make out some vague shapes … the house, the fences that ring the Ranch … and two moving figures are approaching quickly on snowmobiles, their headlights cutting through the darkness. When they pull up, the riders disembark, one man and one woman, though I can't determine who they are.

The woman speaks finally. "You better hurry up, guys, before you turn into popsicles out here! Don't make me freeze my ass off for nothing!"

I'm smiling instantly with the voice, running up to her and hugging her tight. "Aunt Kitty!"

"How ya doin', kid? Come on, we've got a fire started at the house. Fahaian, take Gabe with you."

"Of course, ma'am. Alanna, it is good to see you again." I can't quite see the prince's face, but I can pick out Fahaian's smile in the middle of the hood of his parka as he guides Gabe to his snowmobile. Once everyone's aboard, we motor quickly through the storm toward the Ranch house.

The warmth of the Ranch embraces us both the instant we're in the door. I feel every part of my body starting to thaw. It's a good thing my wings weren't out; they won't have any ice or snow on them and sometimes they take a long time to dry out if they get wet. I take three deep breaths and let my eyes wander around the place, around what I have come to think of as home.

The glow of the fireplace permeates through the darkness of the wintry day, creating orange flickers from one corner of this great room to the other. Several people are huddled in groups around the fire, sharing warm drinks and conversation, sitting at individual tables. Some of these people I recognize from the refuge, clearly taking shelter from the pounding blizzard outside. Others appear to be new residents, probably new supernaturals who have come to find the escape door to Avalon, where Uncle Cyrus has been offering sanctuary from the New Empire.

Then there's one group that I've been eagerly looking for, dead center in front of the fireplace. A very large man, an elderly man, and a teenage girl sit there, surrounding a low coffee table.

God, how I've missed them!

Before I can pipe my voice up to them, though, Aunt Kitty is behind me, bellowing. "We're back, kids, and look who we found auditioning for the role of 'snowman!'"

The group turns around and looks at me. Julian Vibria, the grandfather I didn't know I had until we captured him from an SSA troop last year, his aged eyes smiling more than I recall. Michika Salem, my best friend since we were babies, about to charge and glomp me as usual. Then there's William White Bear … out of all three of these people, I may have missed him the most, just for how much he's come to mean to me. My reverie is abruptly interrupted as Michi literally tackles me into a violent bear hug.

"Alanna! You're back! We've missed you!"

Michi's statement of the obvious notwithstanding, I clutch her tightly and realize that I've missed all of them just as deeply. At this point, I can't help but smile … laugh, even. "It's good to be back, Michi."

She won't release me. This might get awkward after a while, but I look up and find Julian placing a hand on my shoulder. "How have you been, my dear? Staying warm, I hope."

That's odd. Julian doesn't sound like himself.

"I've been okay, splitting time between Canada and Texas. Nobody's been able to catch me yet, thank God."

"Thank the Creator for that, yes." William's voice cuts through the noises around us as he leans over and wraps his arms around both me and Michi … I guess he decided he'd have to hug both of us to get to hug me tonight. William's embrace is punctuated with a soft kiss.

*I've **really** missed that!*

I allow the raw emotion to simply consume me. This is my family, after all … improvised, unusual, but family nonetheless, these are the people that I love. There's only one thing that could make this perfect … two things, really.

Mom and Dad.

January 19th

It took hours for me to get settled in last night, to find my familiar Ranch room with all the trophies, but by the time I fell into that soft bed I was exhausted and ready for sleep. Much of my time was spent with the others, who wanted to know everything about what I'd been doing since last July; where I had gone, how I'd avoided capture, what San Antonio is like in the wintertime. After a while, the time difference and the fatigue of the trip with Gabe caught up with me and I had to excuse myself to get some rest.

This morning, I'm greeted by more friendship and caring. When I open my eyes to greet the day, I realize that I'm not alone in the room. The familiar shadow of William is standing near the door, waiting for me to awaken.

"Good morning, Alanna. I hope we didn't wear you out too much last night."

I rub my eyes gently, sleep threatening to resume its grip on me. "Not too badly, don't worry. What's happening?"

William smiles. I can see his teeth shining through the dim light of the room. "Kitty asked me to get you, to bring you down for breakfast."

I stretch and stand up. Once I have the Sword strapped around my waist, I come back up to William. It still amazes me how massive the man is, how tall and bulked-up he is as he stands before me, waiting for me to join him by his side. There's still the creeping suspicion in the back of my mind that in his transformed state, when he disappears into the wendigo, he will forget about me and threaten me, possibly consume me by giving in to the creature's cannibal nature.

Right now, though, I'm not too worried. I wrap my arms tightly around him. He seems surprised by the gesture. "What's this for?"

I smile up at him, not letting go of his waist for a minute. "Making up for the interrupting Michi." I wink up at him before pulling him down into a longer, more satisfying kiss than we shared last night. He eagerly reciprocates, before we disengage and walk back down the hallway. Even though I'm still in pajamas, thoughtfully loaned to me by Michi, I don't feel too self-conscious around anyone here.

We find our way out into the dining room, surprisingly empty save for a few people hanging around. I'm happy that a couple of the stragglers in the room are Michi and Aunt Kitty. I take a slab of some unusual type of meat ... Aunt Kitty's trademark cuisine ... along with some scrambled eggs and make my way over to the table, placing myself next to Michi. William joins us on the opposite side of the table from me.

"Something's been bugging me all night," Aunt Kitty says to me. "Gabe told us that you'd gone from Traverse City to Montreal, then down to Texas. Didn't you encounter trouble at all on that trip?"

I smile gently, scooping a forkful of eggs into my mouth. "A little bit. It was a nerve-wracking trip, because I wanted to make sure I would avoid any and all air patrols, not an easy thing to do when you can't alight, can't land, and can't speed up without wearing yourself out. I nearly got caught once by a lone plane out of Kentucky, but fortunately enough it was a cloudy day and I had plenty of cover."

Michi has some concern on her face. "So you were, like, full-dragon when you made the trip?"

"I had to be. There was no way just my wings were going to get me that far, I needed the dragon's strength too."

Now it's Aunt Kitty's face I turn to, which shows a slight bit of pride. "You're definitely your mama's little girl, Alanna."

"What do you mean?" William asks.

"Ariel used to do that, carry us for long distances. Though I tell you what, she never hauled ass like *that* at all. At most, she'd fly for six hours straight at a steady pace, which was enough to get us through one border, at least." Aunt Kitty reaches across and tousles my hair. "She'd be proud of you, kid."

"Thanks," I respond with an embarrassed tone. I can feel the blush coming on. It's only stopped when Gabe and Fahaian approach the table, sitting down near us.

Fahaian's sitting on the other side of Michi, a little closer than I'd noticed them being before. There's something going on there, I think.

"Folks, sorry to put a damper on your breakfast, but I thought you'd like some news."

Gabe's words sober us all instantly. He lays down a newspaper in front of us, the most recent New Empire publication from Vancouver. The headline is what gets our attention first.

SUPERNATURAL CELL SENTENCING TODAY: DEATH PENALTY EXPECTED

My brow furrows. "Where is this happening?"

"Salt Lake City. I don't know how much news you've been following …"

None, actually.

"… but this group was picked up by an SSA troop about four months ago. They were the leaders of a large protest group, which had been staging activities outside the state capitol building demanding equal rights for supernaturals."

Aunt Kitty smirks. "There's a great way to put your tit in the wringer."

"That's an understatement. The SSA started files on every member of the group, supernatural or not, and tracked their activities until their next planned protest, when they were all rounded up."

Fahaian chimes in at this point. "The truly bad part of this is that of the ones arrested and tried, none of them are supernatural in any way, shape, or form. During the trial, they were accused of being supernaturals, and in fact their charges were compounded by this."

Gabe nods. "The jury came down with a guilty verdict in less than an hour. They're scheduled to be sentenced this afternoon."

I stroke my chin thoughtfully. "So what does this have to do with us?"

"We're going down there to rescue the group."

Michi's eyes widen. "You mean it?"

"I do. I cleared it with your father, Michika, we're going to allow them to pass through to Avalon."

That reminds me … "Michi, where exactly *is* Uncle Cyrus? I haven't seen him since I got back."

Michi looks kind of sad all of a sudden. "He's in Avalon right now. He felt he was better off at the moment working with the supernaturals that went through already, getting them acclimated."

Aunt Kitty places a hand on my arm. "Alanna, that's none of your concern. And don't believe anyone who tells you we had a fight." The others give Aunt Kitty a blank look. "What?!"

"The point is," Gabe continues, "we're going down to Salt Lake City in two hours."

Now it's my turn to chime in. "How? What kind of transportation do we have that's that fast?"

"It'll be a combined effort. Cyrus is getting ready to move the Ranch again. He'll put us in a good position to act as a base of ops. Once the Ranch has moved, then it's your turn Alanna."

My heart sinks. *He can't be serious, can he?*

"Do you really trust me the way I think you're talking about?"

Gabe nods, very soberly. "We need your abilities. If the dragon was able to fly from Montreal to San Antonio without batting an eyelash, then you for sure can get us to Salt Lake City."

He's serious. He wants the others to ride me to Salt Lake City. Literally.

Chapter Two: Tabernacle

January 19th, continued

I've never been inside the Ranch when Uncle Cyrus casts one of his relocation spells over the place, so I'm not sure what to expect. I see the others around me tying down anything that's loose, which gives me the impression that there's some kind of motion forthcoming. Whatever it is, I hope it's nothing too violent: if anything comes off the walls, anyone underneath would be done for.

We all are tasked with securing loose items with rolls of tape. Pictures, sculptures, trophies, books ... all of them get the Scotch treatment. After about a half hour, we all reassemble in the den area of the Ranch house.

"All set!" Michi calls out to us. "We're secure and ready for transport."

Aunt Kitty nods. "Very well. Gabe, get my husband."

Gabe jogs out of the room for a few minutes. When he returns, he gives me the first glimpse of Uncle Cyrus I've seen since last year.

Is it just me, or is he taller?

His deeply wrinkled face turns up into a smile as he spots me. "Alanna, how wonderful you're back. Just in time for this, as well, I see."

Even if he is a little taller, I still have to crouch to hug the old sorcerer. "Wouldn't have missed it for the world, Uncle Cyrus. I've missed you a lot!"

Uncle Cyrus holds me for a while, until Gabe taps him on the shoulder to remind him of why we need him there. Out of a sidelong glance, I watch how he and Aunt Kitty interact with each other, and I know that something had to have happened: they seem more belligerent than usual toward each other.

"Okay, this time we're only transporting the house. The rest of the Ranch and the refuge are going to stay behind, so we can travel to a smaller piece of real estate." Uncle Cyrus looks around the room. "Everything secure?"

Aunt Kitty nods. "You know it is, Cyrus. Have I let you down yet?"

"Well, it depends …"

"Hey, what the hell is THAT supposed to mean?!" Aunt Kitty is already erupting. This can't be a good sign.

Gabe steps between the two of them. "All right guys, break it up, we've got a job to do. Cyrus, send us, please."

Uncle Cyrus grumbles under his breath as he raises his hands, producing a purple glow which envelops first us, then the entire room, and soon I'm sure the entire house. I feel vibrating in the floor, penetrating through my skeleton and causing me to shift my feet to keep my balance.

I look over at Michi, who sees my distressed expression. "Don't worry, it's always rough at the start." She crosses over to one side of me; William takes the other. It's his first time as well, and he looks like he's in a state of abject panic.

Just as soon as the vibration starts, I get the sensation of my stomach dropping into my shoes. The G-forces must be tremendous to make me queasy … I've been flying really fast as the dragon lately, so I thought I'd be used to it by now. Just as suddenly, my guts whip up into my throat as we hit a fast descent, threatening my gag reflex.

Michi has her arms up in the air, like she's riding the world's biggest roller coaster. Why am I not surprised by that? William, on the other hand, has a death grip on my shoulder, grinding his teeth. I squeeze my eyes shut, anticipating the hard impact to come.

Fortunately, it never does. The landing is pillow-soft, the vibration quick to cease afterward. Once I regain my equilibrium, I look around at the others, then to Uncle Cyrus. "Where are we now?"

He smiles, a little fatigued. Maybe he's shrunk again; he seems smaller than he was when I saw him before the trip. "A little, forgotten corner of Arches National Park. No hikers come back here, especially not at this time of year. Just be careful when you open the door, because it's a nature preserve and I don't want to cause more damage than necessary."

We all acknowledge Uncle Cyrus's warning, heading for the door. What awaits us outside is stunning, the vistas and doorways of the park are right there outside the house. Were this not for such an important matter, I'd be inclined to remain at the house and admire the scenery, maybe fly through some of the arches to stretch my wings.

Gabe's hand on my shoulder sobers me from my admiration of the scene. "It's time, Alanna."

I nod and walk outside, unstrapping the Sword from my waist and relocating it on my arm. I'll need it there once this transformation is finished. I close my eyes, crouch down on all fours in the Utah dirt, and focus my concentration into my own body, willing myself to become more than I am.

Coaxing the dragon out of her den.

My arms lengthen. My torso bulks and stretches, straining the clothes I wear, but thankfully not breaching them. My wings unfurl and grow along with my other limbs and my neck. Fire burns in my belly, ready to be called into action when I need it. The belt of the Sword's sheath, once loose around my forearm, tightens as the muscles grow, as the bones harden and bulk up. My face is always the last part of the transformation, and finally I feel the deforming of my mouth and nose, stretching me, making me more reptilian with every passing moment. Once everything is stretched to its limits, I return my attention to my surroundings.

Where I once stood as a teenage girl, now a dragon occupies the space. As I've spent my months in hiding, I've tried to learn all I can about my transformations, this new form I can take, and everything Mom knew about flight. It's been quite an education, but now is when it's going to pay off.

I lift a taloned forefoot off the ground and motion toward the others. *"Time to get aboard."*

Gabe nods toward me and motions for the others to join him. One by one William, Michi, and Fahaian scale my arm and settle in on my shoulders. Gabe is the last to climb up, and he goes one step further than the others by straddling my neck. *I'm glad this form is really strong, because Gabe is insanely heavy for some reason ...*

Gabe motions again to the door, where Aunt Kitty and Uncle Cyrus now stand watching us depart. "Keep a careful eye out guys, I'm pretty sure the park rangers aren't connected to the SSA, but you can never be too sure. We should be back before nightfall."

Aunt Kitty waves at us. "Dinner will be waiting, kids!"

Gabe pats the side of my neck, as close as he can get to my flank. "Okay, Alanna, let's go. Northwest, best speed."

I stretch my wings. I haven't let the dragon out of me since I got to San Antonio, so she's a little rusty in the flight department, but after a couple of experimental flaps I think I'm ready to lift off, the joints of my wings properly stretched. I flap my wings hard ... once ... twice ... on the third flap I leap off the ground and take to the air, flapping harder to maintain my altitude, until I've climbed up through the low clouds of the day and the Ranch house is no longer in sight. I level off at a good altitude for my passengers, around 12,000 feet, before I slow my wing flaps down and start riding the air currents.

"Everybody okay up there?"

I'm convinced that the wind has whipped my voice away from the others, but soon I hear a reply from William. "We're all good. Michika's a little cold, but Fahaian's got her covered!"

I can only imagine what that might imply. Satisfied that everyone's still with me, I focus on the job at hand, getting us to Salt Lake City. It doesn't take long before the Great

Salt Lake is approaching on the horizon: through the breaks in the clouds I can see first the city, then the massive lake beyond it. I lower us slightly, just below the clouds.

That's a mistake.

I see the aircraft blow past us before I'm fully aware of what's happening. Then the sonic boom hits me, and jars me off course. Fighter planes, two of them, bright blue.

The Supernatural Suppression Agency. The SSA no doubt is using the old U.S. Air Force resources now.

They're coming back around. No doubt they've spotted me and are regrouping to attack. The fire is gurgling in my guts. Without any worries about doing it while carrying passengers, I open my mouth and allow the gurgling to erupt in a flaming streak, hurtling toward one of the planes. The fire lightly bounces off of the fuselage before making contact with something combustible and causing the jet to erupt in a massive ball of destruction. No parachute appears.

We don't want to kill the pawns, I remind my dragon self. *Only the ones in charge.*

The second plane begins its attack run, firing a machine gun at us. Without thinking again I barrel-roll to avoid the bullets, forgetting that I'm carrying human cargo on my back. I feel eight hands grip my flesh tighter as I drop into a dive, narrowly avoiding more bullets.

The jet has all of the advantages on me. It's far faster than I can fly as the dragon. It's better armed: all I have is fire. It has threat warning systems which give the pilot a heads-up on where attackers are, while all I have is my wits.

Will that be enough?

I unfurl my wings and return to climbing, flapping them hard. I feel one hand releasing my shoulder, a slender, feminine hand.

Michi's going to try a spell. Better brace myself.
"CONCUSSION!"

A heavy burst of energy shoots forth from Michi's hand. The recoil is too much, however, and it throws me backward into a free fall. I wasn't ready for that, and now I'm paying the price, hurtling down to the ground in an uncontrolled spin, fighting the wind to open my wings again. I can look up and see the spell's results, as the jet she fired at is in much the same boat as I am, in a tailspin unable to pull up.

Fat lot of good that does me *right now.*

I need to locate the others. I can't feel them on my back. Quickly I scan the air around me. Gabe to my right. William in front of me. Fahaian and Michi, clinging to each other, on my left. I question briefly whether I'm large enough to reach all of them before making my decision. My right hand stretches and grabs Gabe. Fahaian and Michi are just out of reach of my left, but Fahaian grabs my finger and pulls himself and Michi into my grip.

I stretch my neck as far as it will go and grasp William in my jaws.

With everyone collected and with me, I try to regain control of my body. I look down, still in spinning free fall.

The ground's too close! I can't pull up!

I spread my wings and try to flap up. No response, plus they feel like they've been seriously injured. I can smell blood coming from them.

We're all going to die—

"Alanna, use your fire!"

The words come from Fahaian. He wants me to firecast, but how? How do I do it without barbecuing William in my mouth?

"Trust me!" Fahaian touches his nose. I think I get it now.

I keep my mouth clamped shut around William. The fire churns in my gut. With all my concentration on the ground fast approaching, I blow fire through my nostrils toward the ground. It burns like hell!

Fahaian has his lighter out. He flicks the flame on. The next thing I know, all of us are only one foot off of the ground, from our previous height that was immeasurable, the result of Fahaian's telepyretic abilities; he must have zapped us to the ground through my fire and his lighter.. We hit the ground very hard, but not hard enough to kill us. My grip on my friends tightens.

I hear Michi whooping. It must have worked. "Awesome! Let's do that again!"

"I'd prefer not to," Gabe mutters sardonically from my other hand. I open my mouth and allow William, now slightly soggy with dragon slobber, to exit. I release my grip on Gabe and set him on the ground.

I nearly do the same for Fahaian and Michi, until I notice the pose they're in. Michi has herself wrapped around Fahaian and has him trapped in a liplock. The prince's face, adorably, shows his combination of shock, confusion, and enjoyment.

They can't enjoy the moment, though, because sirens fill the air around us. More SSA, this time ground troops, arrive and surround us, the blueshirted soldiers pouring forth from their vehicles. I look all around us and see that there are at least twelve cars circling us, with four times as many men.

"Buy me time, Gabe!"

"We'll give you all we can. Let's go, guys!" Gabe leads the others into the fight. The battle rages all around me as I focus my concentration on shrinking back down, on reclaiming my human form. Once I feel my wings withdraw into my back, I look up and see my friends are outgunned and being pushed back.

Time to change the score. I stand up and draw the Sword. The closing of the armor around my body is starting to become more of a comfort, as I know I will have the paladin's strength and power backing up my friends. In mere seconds, the Guardswoman stands in the midst of the fight, Sword at the ready. I launch into a quick sprint toward the blueshirts.

Control has been my Achilles heel as the Guardswoman. Now I only wonder, after not letting her out for months, will I be able to control the power?

Some of the blueshirts are already retreating, getting back in their cars. A few of them are continuing to fight, and it's become apparent that a couple of them, a man and a woman, are supernaturals, just judging by the scars they wear on their foreheads. I thrust the Sword into the woman's head and watch the blade pass through, catching the small silicon chip that was controlling her and extracting it from her brain. Once the chip is clear, she turns on the other blueshirts and uses her powers ... apparently something to do with cold, because many of the blueshirts are shivering and developing frosty coverings on their uniforms.

While she distracts them, and Michi handles the other human pawns, I turn my attention to the supernatural male blueshirt. He's going to be harder to liberate ... his power seems to be coating him head-to-toe in some sort of natural armor, like an insect exoskeleton. He has long, roach-like arms which he swats at the Sword with. I unfurl my wings, feeling the slight pain in their injuries, and try to get an advantage by flapping over him: this seems to do the trick, as I'm able to vertically drive the Sword into the chip scar and extract his chip that way.

When the device is free of his brain, Roach-man, like his female counterpart, shakes his head like he's been in a fog for a while. I land and sheathe the Sword. The migraine I'd gotten used to, for some reason, isn't coming now. *Maybe I'm getting used to the role.*

"Are you going to hurt us?" Roach-man's voice tremulously asks me.

"Not a chance. We're going to offer you an escape."

Cold-girl, standing by Michi and Fahaian, smiles over at us. "Thank you, miss ... we don't know how long we've been missing."

William and Gabe join our group finally, with Gabe taking the lead. "If you don't mind our asking, do you know anything about the sentencing in the city today?"

Roach-man nods. "We were supposed to be on that security detail, except we got called out to fight you guys instead."

"They're being transported from City Hall to the Temple," Cold-girl continues.

This seems very odd to me. "Why would they do something like that?"

Roach-man shrugs. "It confused us too ... there was some kind of weak explanation, that it was going to demonstrate exactly how much God hates supernaturals or something ..."

Gabe's face grows grim. "If there's one thing the Regents *cannot* do, it's speak for God." He approaches Cold-girl and places a hand on her shoulder. "How soon are they being moved?"

She shivers slightly under Gabe's hand. "Actually ... it'd be right now. They're en-route, and should be at the Temple in about ten minutes."

"That gives us too little time!" William's voice is urgent. I can see he's already starting to deform, starting to let the wendigo out.

"Alanna, how are you doing wing-wise?"

I unfurl my wings and flap them. Sharp, stabbing pain forces me to retract them again. "Not good, Gabe, I can't fly like this."

"We'll have to drive, then." He turns quickly to Michi. "Take these two back to the Ranch house. We'll take care of the SSA caravan."

Roach-man tosses Gabe a set of keys. "Take my cruiser."

"Thanks." Gabe smiles and ushers us over to the car that Roach-man points toward. Once we're all in, I look in the mirror as Michi and the two liberated supernaturals wink out of sight, no doubt headed back to the house.

When I look back over at Gabe, though, his face shows his worry. "What is it?"

Gabe's teeth are grinding. "If they're going to condemn those people in a House of God, then the nation's corruption will be complete. We absolutely must stop this from happening."

William and Fahaian lean forward, but it's Fahaian who speaks. "I thought this nation had already been completely corrupted."

"Very close to it, but not quite. If they do what I think they're going to do inside the Temple, then it will complete the corruption, and we'll be completely on our own, in terms of … shall we say, divine intervention."

Gabe closes his hand around his cell phone, looking a little worried. His foot pushes down on the accelerator, and we speed toward what could be a defining battle that could either save some lives or damn us all.

Chapter Three: Reception

January 19th, continued

Gabe is an accomplished driver. I learned this last year when he was driving us all around the country looking for my dad. Even that, though, didn't hold a candle for the job he's doing now, speeding us through the streets of Salt Lake City.

Our bodies fling against the walls of the car as Gabe takes hard turns without letting up on the gas. A couple times, I feel like the wheels come off the ground on one side, and we're bound to be rolling over soon. The six SSA cars chasing us aren't helping, either.

Gabe makes a motion back toward the guys, sitting in the back seat. "William, Fahaian, you guys are going to have to give us a distraction. We need to get those guys off our tail."

I roll down the window and shoot flames out of my mouth toward the rear, but I have no way of aiming: I don't know if I hit the cars or if I hit pedestrians. William, on the other hand, is not quite as gentle with our car: he grows into the wendigo quickly once the gunfire starts, kicking out one of the back doors and leaping out of the car to confront our pursuers by himself. I can hear crunching metal, but that sound is obscured by William's loud, inhuman roars.

Don't look back, Alanna. Just trust yourself not to look back.

Fahaian, meanwhile, taps me on the shoulder. "If we stay, will you two be all right?"

"We will," I respond.

"Just go now!" Gabe screams. Fahaian nods and leaps out of the car himself, rolling as he hits the pavement until he's on his feet and ready to fight.

My attention is already back forward, as Gabe's driving lifts all four tires off the road, taking a slight hill. The car screeches back down and continues on its way toward our goal, the large Temple at the center of the city.

Even as we speed along, it gives me time to ponder the questions in my mind. Why would the New Empire commandeer the Temple for an execution? Unless the Regents suddenly had a sense of religion ... which, if Gabe's comment is to be believed, they don't ... there must be some reason why they would want to carry out the sentence there.

Wait ... Gabe mentioned something about this ... *"we'll be completely on our own, in terms of ... shall we say, divine intervention."*

I look over to Gabe. "Is there something you need to tell me?"

He groans. "Now is not the time for this, Alanna ..."

"Make the time, Gabe. Why does the New Empire want to execute people in the Temple? You seem really agitated about it."

I can hear his teeth grind over the screaming car engine. "If they're allowed to do that, then the remaining good citizens of the New Empire are as good as lost. At the least, the nation will have been turned away from the vision of God." He grips the steering wheel tighter. "Numerous nations have done this before. Many of them had this pattern, this sequence of events which has taken place. The Regents are replicating the pattern, almost exactly."

I don't think I can handle the details right now. I simply clutch a Jesus handle along the car's ceiling and hang on for the ride, which thankfully isn't much further as the Temple is coming into sight.

Along with six more SSA vehicles, three police cars, and about fifty blueshirts.

Gabe slides the car sideways to a screeching halt, which flings me out of the passenger seat and through the open window.

Just like I wanted. I unfurl my wings, trying to hide my pain as their injured webbing expands, and draw the Sword. The Guardswoman flaps her way into battle once again.

These blueshirts are almost exclusively human pawns, thankfully, so it does not take much to knock them out of the fight. I cut my way through the sea of blue, working my way toward the steps of the Temple, even as more pawns arrive and try to stop me. The Guardswoman's strength is too much for them, leaving them sprawling either on the steps or in the courtyard.

My heart starts to race, just as I've knocked over another six blueshirts. *Oh God ... he's here.* The control I thought I had over the Guardswoman starts to falter, as I let her divine the location of her one greatest nemesis, pulling me along for the ride, until finally he stands before us, at the top of the steps leading to the Temple entrance.

General Tyrelius Scolar, Chairman of the Joint Chiefs of Staff, field commander of the SSA. The holder of a Sabre which houses the hellish Invader paladin.

My father.

I don't want to fight him. I've dreaded this encounter for six months, feared what would occur should we cross paths again. I don't want to kill him. He's my daddy, after all.

The Guardswoman assumes her *en garde* stance. Scolar smirks ... the eye shields he wore last year are completely gone, so I can see his entire scarred face curl up when he emotes. His hand goes for the Sabre, but then stops.

"I don't think so today, Sharpe. I'm under orders."

Why won't he draw? What's wrong? The Guardswoman seethes, but does not attack. I resume my control over her, forcing her to sheathe the Sword. I pull my wings back into myself and approach cautiously, my eyes focused on the man.

"I don't want to fight you, Dad."

He laughs. "Going soft? Far from a proper Guardsman, aren't you?"

I grit my teeth. "Somewhere in that brain is Cole Sharpe … Daddy, come out, I need you!"

Scolar spits on the step he stands on. "Meaningless, hatchling. There's no Cole Sharpe. He's dead." He lowers his voice. "I killed him."

I can't believe what he's saying. Not when I'm this close … not when I can hear his muttering, hear the name he keeps repeating like a nervous tic.

"Ariel." *My mom's name.*

I hear Scolar's radio crackle to life. He puts a finger up to his ear. "Scolar here … Understood. I'm on my way." He turns his attention back to me. "It seems that our reunion is cut short, Sharpe. Our work here is done."

A chill goes down my spine. *The prisoners … the execution …*

Scolar calmly walks down the stairs, toward my position. I'm frozen to the spot, like my feet are glued to the ground. When he's close enough, he whispers into my ear.

"You'll be next, my girl … but on *my* terms … I will take down yet another Guardsman … yet another Sharpe."

He laughs. His breath, layered with God knows what odors, lingers as he steps away and continues down the stairs. A man wailing is the next sound I hear, and I run up the stairs toward the source.

When I reach the entrance of the Temple, I find a man carrying out another man … a very *dead* man, apparently stabbed through the heart. The carrier, an older, graying man apparently in his 60's, is the one who is wailing, clutching the younger dead man to his chest. I step aside to allow him to pass by. Behind him, six more impromptu pallbearers carry out six more bodies … two more men and four women … all of them with similar injuries. A bloody trail is left by the procession.

At the tail end of it, face ashen, is Gabe. I rush over to his side as he collapses to his knees, tossing one of his arms over my shoulders.

"Gabe, what happened?"

His voice quavers. "We were too late. I ran inside only to witness the last one ..." He clutches his cell phone, opens it, and gives it to me. "Now look."

I take the phone from him, look at the screen, and my stomach bottoms out. The message flashes cruelly, bright yellow against a black backdrop.

NO SIGNAL

I shiver as I carry the agent back to our ruined car. No signal. No way to contact Gabe's Employer.

We're now truly on our own.

January 21ˢᵗ

The information has been sitting on my heart ever since I saw the message on the phone. Sharing it has been no help, to me or to anyone.

The first ones we told were Fahaian and William, who took it fairly neutrally. They understand, though, and are ready to stand with us. Michi and her parents, on the other hand ... I think Aunt Kitty's going to be spending the next week or so replacing all the drywall she destroyed in her tirade. Hope seems to be in short supply right now.

About the only hope we have lies in the recently-liberated supernatural blueshirts, who've finally given us their names ... which is much better than calling them Cold-girl and Roach-man. Hopefully these two will be like Jerry Tile last year, friendly and happy to be free, and not the second coming of Yolanda French, the deep-cover agent who nearly killed me twice.

It's Cold-girl ... or rather, Teresa Iles ... who snaps me out of my meditative state, staring out at the arches from the front door of the house. "Gabe needs you in the other room, Alanna."

I nod and thank her, following her inside. Teresa, by necessity, still wears her SSA uniform, but to the relief of all of us here Michi changed the color of the fabric so that it's not a reminder of the enemy. In Teresa's case, now the shirt's yellow.

She tries to strike up a conversation with me, even though I feel like the worst kind of company right now. "How many others have you rescued?"

I shrug. "A few, at least. We didn't even know there were supernatural blueshirts until last year, so it kind of shifted our missions a little bit." The silence looms over us as we walk, so I have to break it. "How did they get you guys?"

"I don't know exactly how they got Trent, but as far as me, I guess it's because I was too trusting of some supernaturals I'd gone to college with."

This has my interest now. "What do you mean?"

"One of my closest college friends got me involved with a protest group, some kind of supernatural-rights organization who was arranging college campus protests of the New Empire. She even marched with us a few times. Only it turned out she was a double agent, and she was supposed to lead the SSA to us. When they came, they locked me up, they tortured me, and then things get a little fuzzy."

I nod knowingly. Some of the folks who have been freed from the blueshirts tell us that their memories of their SSA time are nearly completely gone following the removal of the control chips. "Do you remember much of anything?"

Teresa sighs. "Bits and pieces. It's mostly restricted to the last couple of months, our orders and such. I don't know how much help that'll be to you and your friends."

I place a hand on Teresa's arm, slowing her up slightly. "Believe me, any information you can give us is going to be helpful. And we'll get you out of country as soon as possible, okay?"

She smiles, kind of relieved, I think. "Thank you."

We continue deeper into the house, until we reach the room where the others sit, the long dining hall. Steaming coffee aromas fill the air and engulf us as we approach: obviously Gabe is doubling-down on his usual habit as a coping mechanism. He doesn't exactly look great, considering that his phone went dead.

Then again Mom's told me Who's on the other end of that line.

The others are lightly snacking, keeping all of their eyes on Roach-man, who finally identified himself to us as Trent Gracin. Teresa breaks off from my side and goes to the other side to sit next to Trent. It's only after I sit down between Michi and William that I notice the two former blueshirts are holding hands.

Trent seems to understand my confused expression. "You're wondering about this?" He squeezes Teresa's hand slightly tighter with his insectoid claws.

"Maybe a little," I respond. "Teresa, is this one of those past-month memories you were talking about?"

She shrugs. "I don't really know, Alanna. Once the chips were gone, we still had some connection on an emotional level. It's very nice that we were both liberated at the same time ... it allows us to stay together no matter what."

True love, even in the face of torment. Don't I know a little about that! Under the table, I place a hand lightly on William's thigh, trying to reassure myself and him that we have something like Teresa and Trent appear to.

Gabe clears his throat, only after polishing off what appears to be a quart-size cup of coffee, apparently all in one swallow. "Okay folks, here's what we know right now. One, we're cut off from any kind of divine help, thanks to the actions two days ago in the city. Two, Scolar was with the group conducting the execution. Three, Kitty tells me that Cyrus was injured during the transportation of the Ranch house, so we can't reunite with the others for at least a month. That leaves us here, in hiding. Any ideas that you have will be more than welcome, since I'm kind of tapped out right now." He refills his mug.

Michi clears her throat. "Anyone else we can contact, other than your Employer?"

Gabe shakes his head. "It's going to be damned hard to. Without a signal on this network, I can't even contact anyone like Durga."

"Not that it's much of a tragedy," Aunt Kitty bitterly mutters. Her feelings about the Hindu goddess notwithstanding, the thought of not being able to contact Durga makes me a little frightened, as she became a great help to both me and William by training us.

Wait … something Gabe said gives me a glimmer of hope. "You said 'damned hard,' not 'impossible.' There are other contact methods?"

Gabe shrugs. "Certain figures are going to be out of contact because they use the network exclusively, but others can be reached the old-fashioned way … through prayer or, if we can connect back with the rest of the Ranch, through the Avalon doorway."

That's better than nothing, if we can hold out for the month it'll take Uncle Cyrus to recover. "It's a shot, at least."

Gabe sighs, a little resigned to my positivity. "Okay then, if you say so." He turns to Trent and Teresa. "Do you have any recollection of your SSA time other than your relationship?"

Both of them get very thoughtful, intense looks on their faces, like they're racking their memories for some nugget. Trent clears his throat before finally responding. "I can give you as many particulars as I can. The main thing is that we had a number of higher-ups camping with our troop in the last couple of months, in anticipation of the execution."

William, who obviously makes Trent uncomfortable to be in the general vicinity, rumbles, "which higher-ups? Do you have names?"

Teresa answers before Trent. "The biggest one was General Scolar. He'd been with us in Flagstaff for a while."

Dad, you were so close to home ... "Is that your troop's base?" I ask before thinking.

Trent nods. "We were both taken from around the area by the SSA, so they put us back there, kind of as some sort of bureaucratic irony I guess."

A chill runs up my spine. *Dad's still in Scolar, he's fighting it ... he's got to be ...*

"Who else was with you?" Michi's question breaks the uncomfortable silence.

"Mostly mid-level commanders," Trent responds. "Three administrators came from D.C. as the General's entourage, I guess to keep him in touch with the Capitol. I do recall he took three calls from Vice President Regent while he was with us."

Fahaian, who sits on the other side of Michi from me, strokes his chin. "This is interesting ... Alanna, Gabe, do you see the opportunity here?"

We all look confusedly over at the crown prince of Jordan. Gabe pipes up, "I don't follow."

"Don't you see? If one Regent directly contacts General Scolar, that must mean he has an inside track to their side. If we can find a way to exploit that, we can bring a swift conclusion to this struggle."

He wants us to go on the offensive. *To do that, though ...*

Aunt Kitty facepalms loud enough for us to hear the impact. "Don't you know the first goddamn thing about strategy, kid? How in the *fuck* are we going to be able to use Scolar's inside track, if we can't get Scolar with us?"

She has a point, but the simplicity of Fahaian's idea is catching. Before I can stop myself, I respond to Aunt Kitty's question. "We capture Scolar."

Now all the attention's on me, with a lot of faces that show disbelief. William has a hand on my cheek suddenly. "Alanna, are you okay?"

"I'm fine, don't worry about me." I take William's hand in mine. "I haven't been thinking clearer about the man until now. We capture Scolar. We get our inside track. We go to Washington unimpeded." I shoot a glance at Gabe. "We get Mom."

Gabe shoots a concerned look toward me. "Are you positive you want to do this? You know what happened the last time you went out looking for Scolar … are you ready for what you might discover?"

My heart's in my throat now. Memories rush back in a flood.

The duel.

The fire around us, the building coming down.

The Sword taking the Invader's helmet off, only to reveal Dad underneath.

I swallow hard. I can't let the others see how nervous this makes me. "Absolutely. There's no other way, as far as I can see." I look around at the others. "Are you in, or out?"

William clutches my shoulders gently. "To the end, Alanna, I'm with you."

Michi takes my hand. "Me too. You can't get rid of me that easy."

"As am I," Fahaian responds.

Though I barely know them, Trent and Teresa lean forward. "We'll give you all the help we can, Ms. Sharpe. Whatever you need, we'll do it."

Aunt Kitty seems a bit more hesitant, but finally appears to relent. "Since I'm outvoted, I guess I'll join the cool kids. *Some*body's gotta watch out for you guys, after all."

We all turn back toward Gabe, expectantly. He takes a long sip from his coffee mug. When he sets it down, his face is back to being the Gabe of old … controlled, cool, unflappable Gabe.

"All right then. But we're doing this the *right* way this time, Alanna. We're making a plan first."

Chapter Four: Subterfuge

February 1st

Planning takes too long. I want out of this place now.

The group of us, still stuck deep in the recesses of Arches, can't agree on a plan of attack for our attempt to capture Scolar. Trent and Teresa veto every idea we've thought up for the last nearly two weeks. While they're probably right to, since they were the ones who were blueshirts and probably have a better idea of their tactics, it's still aggravating.

The couple has, though, given us a better idea of what tends to surround the General. He has a group of retainers that regularly follows him. Three of them are bureaucrats, no combat skills at all: they handle all the paperwork for Scolar's activities. He has two very large bodyguards, who usually train the troop the General camps with when they're not killing anyone who gets close to him. Possibly most important, though, is the one SSA soldier who acts as his personal assistant, which means carrying his phone. That information's causing us to change our plans, because if we're going to use Scolar as an in to the White House, we'll need that soldier as well.

Now we're simply stuck on where to go and how to attack. Trent had a schedule committed to memory of Scolar's activities, which he now only half-remembers without his control chip. Teresa was never privy to the General's travel plans, so she's no help at all in this regard. We sit around the dining room table for the umpteenth time in the last week, trying to determine where to go.

"Now, you're sure about that schedule?" Gabe levelly asks.

"I am," Trent responds. "After leaving Salt Lake, he was supposed to go back to Flagstaff. Then he's supposed to be on a troop inspection trip near the MRZ, followed by some sort of personal day in Virginia before heading back to Washington."

Aunt Kitty settles further into her seat. "Should we try to get him on the way to the MRZ?"

Fahaian raises his eyebrow. "I apologize, if I may ask what 'the MRZ?' is"

Gabe uncomfortably shifts in his seat. "It's short for 'Missouri Rad Zone.' We had to evacuate the entire state after a chain of nuclear reactor meltdowns, triggered by an earthquake. There's a wall currently erected on land, and three filtering stations which cross the Mississippi River at the Zone's eastern border."

Fahaian nods, and then gains a questioning expression. "Why do they keep troops there? It doesn't seem like a tactical advantage to place soldiers where no one will come to fight."

We exchange brief glances, but eventually it's Gabe who answers, again. "Some of the residents of Missouri … before it became the Zone … manifested their supernatural states after the meltdowns. The Regents decided to wall off the state after it was evacuated, but …"

Fahaian's eyebrows rise. I guess I'll finish the explanation. "They left those supernaturals in the Zone, quarantined them from the rest of the population, and those guards watch over the Zone to make sure they don't escape. The best guess is they're hoping the radiation levels will do the work for the SSA."

Before anyone can say anything else, Aunt Kitty aims a stern look at both me and Fahaian. "Don't even think about it. There are no guarantees you guys can even find those supernaturals alive, let alone get out of the MRZ yourselves."

I wish she couldn't read my mind like that!

"Nevertheless," Gabe interjects, "the idea has merit. We can intercept Scolar and party when they inspect the troops at the MRZ." He strokes his chin thoughtfully. "Actually, we might have an in with the base itself. Kitty, I believe you know one of the commanders."

"I do?" Aunt Kitty seems surprised, but then her expression changes. It's worried. I've never seen her worry about anything ... a trait Michi inherited from her mom. "You don't mean who I think you do. You can't."

Gabe nods. "I do, actually. He's been there for a while. The higher-ups don't seem to like him too much ... you can imagine why."

This conversation of half-statements has everyone else's full attention. I guess our faces demand an explanation, which Aunt Kitty finally offers. "I ... might ... maybe ... have a friend who's #3 at the MRZ base."

William leans closer. "Will he help us?"

"I'm sure he will, I served with him in my first command. While we really didn't keep in touch, I know he'll remember me."

Michi looks hurt. "Why haven't you told me about this before, Mom?"

Aunt Kitty shrugs. "I never got around to it?" Her sheepish grin isn't helping the situation.

Gabe finally makes the decision. "Call him up, Kitty. The rest of us are going to prepare."

February 8ᵗʰ

I hate this uniform. I hate looking over at that wall and pondering the slow and agonizing death of people behind it. I hate having to march around with all of these blueshirts and look like I belong. I hate this whole situation ... but if it'll get me Scolar, then I'll deal with it.

Aunt Kitty really does have a friend who's the third-in-command at this base, who she introduced to us as Warrant Officer Pete Lonstein. She eventually had to tell us the whole story, that Lonstein had been her second in command on her first SEAL mission in command. He was surprised to hear from her, from what she told us, but agreed to help mainly because his association with Aunt Kitty has left him with a precarious position in the SSA, so he feels that he's got nothing to lose by helping us sneak in.

I'm still not sure if Gabe's idea is the best one. He had Uncle Cyrus, still recuperating, generate a bunch of fake SSA uniforms for all of us, so that we could integrate with the blueshirts there and not all have to rely on Holographic Self-Image Projectors. As it was, I was the only one who got one of the devices so that I could hide the Sword, but I'd prefer not to have to wear the uniform all the same. Teresa, it turns out, was studying theater makeup when she was taken, so she is able to manufacture control chip scars for everyone who doesn't have HoSIPs, making it appear that we've all been through the Traverse City hell camp. Once properly disguised, we set out for the MRZ, and just got here yesterday.

Now I'm marching with a bunch of other blueshirts … human pawns, all … patrolling along the wall which defends Kansas City from the atomic wasteland that Missouri has become. None of the other blueshirts even talk to me. That's good, because I don't even want to deal with questions as to where I came from, who I am, or what my aspirations might be.

They really won't like the answer …

"Vibria! Front and center, soldier!"

It takes me a second to remember that I'm the one being called … as far as these blueshirts are concerned, my name is Irene Vibria. I break off from the patrolling formation and run over to the owner of the voice, one Sergeant Vick. I square up and salute. "Sir!"

He slaps my arm down. "Don't salute me, dumbass, I'm a non-com! Don't you remember boot?" Vick groans and rubs his nose. "Never mind. Join up with Bravo Company, you're on VIP duty with them. Some higher-ups from DC are coming today, and they're shorthanded."

I don't want to get swatted again, so I nod. "Yes, Sergeant." I run in the direction Vick motions toward, trying to conceal my eagerness.

Higher-ups from DC. Commanders. *Scolar* ...

My wandering mind has replaced my situational awareness, and as a result I nearly run into Bravo Company's sergeant, a woman about my size with a shrill, commanding voice.

"What is your problem, soldier? Square up, damn it!"

I strike what I think is an attentive pose. "Private Irene Vibria, I was sent here from Echo Company by Sgt. Vick."

"Figures, Vick sends me someone as green as you. Very well, find a space and fall in. The VIPs are en-route, e.t.a. 5 minutes."

"Yes, Sergeant," I pipe up before finding my way over to where the rest of Bravo company stands, waiting for the caravan. Discipline seems to be a bit looser in Bravo, as these blueshirts mull about and talk amongst each other.

I see a silhouette I recognize, and make my way through the crowd until I'm next to a particular blueshirt, standing extremely tall amongst the others. I hope that my voice blends in with the others as I stage whisper up to him. "William!"

He turns and finds me standing next to him. "I thought you were with Echo Company."

"I was, but Vick sent me over here. Is it who I'm thinking it is?"

William, in his disguise as a blueshirt named "Zeke Rooney," nods slowly in confirmation. "His entire entourage. They're stopping here for the troop inspection."

I nod and reach toward my hip. While I can feel the Sword, still hanging from my hip, most other observers probably only see me dropping my arm slightly away from my right leg. I don't spend too much time mulling over how awkward my pose must be, because a large black SUV pulls up to the front of Bravo Company. From my perspective I can barely see the proceedings …

… but I feel them in my gut. I feel it as soon as the door opens, as soon as I hear the company's sergeant call us to attention. It's difficult, but I snap to attention and salute, along with the others, keeping up the ruse.

Through a part in the troops, I watch Scolar return the sergeant's salute. She clicks her heels together and assumes a ramrod position. "General Scolar, sir, Bravo company of SSA Troop 482, Kansas City division, welcomes you to the MRZ."

Scolar turns toward the rest of the company after the sergeant barks out an order arms command. The general's eyes narrow.

He feels me too …

"Sergeant, have you had any new additions to this company?"

The sergeant has a questioning look. "Sir?"

"I'm not entirely convinced that your entire unit is who you think."

Crap, he's on to our trick …

"I did have a couple soldiers come down with flu a couple of days ago, they're in the infirmary. I have one from Echo and one from Tango to make up my company's numbers. They'll be dismissed as soon as my boys are given the okay by the doctor."

My heart is racing. I watch the General and his two aides slowly push their way between soldiers, making way toward us. *He knows …*

He's right between myself and William. He turns away from me, thankfully. "Identify, soldier."

William appears to straighten up taller. "Private Zeke Rooney, Tango company, sir!"

Scolar eyeballs William, poring over him with scrutiny that makes me very nervous. Apparently he spots the fake scar on his head, so he accepts him as legitimate.

Now his attention's on me. Oh God …

"And you, soldier? Identify."

I can't seem nervous. I straighten up like William did. "Private Irene Vibria, Echo company, sir!"

Scolar's eyes narrow. He looks up and down my body. "Something wrong with your arm, Vibria?"

Damn! "It's an old injury, sir. Threw out my shoulder playing softball and it didn't heal correctly, sir."

His eyes get a sinister glint. "Let me help you, then." His voice is dripping with venomous intent. He reaches for my right wrist … the one with the HoSIP …

Someone above us has figured out that the whole thing has quickly gone to hell on us. A shot rings out from overhead, hitting the side glass of the General's SUV. Everyone ducks except for me, Scolar, and William, even as another shot drops one of the General's aides.

Scolar growls at me and squeezes my wrist tightly, effectively wrecking the HoSIP. My camouflage body drops very suddenly, and it's just me standing there in a blueshirt uniform, Sword dangling from my hip.

Public enemy number one, out in the open and vulnerable.

"My terms, Sharpe. You die now!" Scolar draws the Sabre of the Invader. The armor closes around him, yet he never releases my wrist. He's holding it so tightly against my body, in a death grip so secure that I can't draw …

Mother, I'm sorry.

The Invader is yanked away suddenly and thrown against his truck. The other troops scatter in a panic as gunshots continue to rain down, taking out the other aide, but the Invader returns to his feet, narrowing his eyes through the faceplate of his death's-head helmet.

"So … you brought friends to die for you!" He clutches the Sabre in both hands and rushes for William, still in mid-transformation. I pull the Sword from its sheath and feel the

transformation begin, even as a stabbing pain punches all the way up my right arm, the arm Scolar had a grip on. I can't even close my right hand … so I'm stuck fighting one-handed. I swing the Sword between the Invader and William, backing the hell knight off. I assume the best *en garde* stance I can manage, the Sword slightly off-balance in my left hand. The Invader charges and I parry his swings very loosely, keeping myself between him and William.

Trying to, at least, until William leaps over my head and tackles the Invader. The Sabre clatters out of his hand, leaving Scolar lying on the ground beneath the wendigo, whose mouth dribbles on his pressed uniform.

"You think this will stop me?" Scolar's voice is a strained sneer, but his words have weight as he pulls his gun out of its holster. Trying to stop him from firing, I throw the Sword between the two of them, striking Scolar's hand just as the pistol goes off.

William yelps and scrambles off of the General. He curls up into a furry, white ball, trying to get away from the fight as quickly as possible. My useless right arm trailing behind me, I run to recover the Sword before Scolar gets any bright ideas … Scolar is doing the same for his own weapon. On the run I collect the hilt in my hand, and the armor's fully closed around me by the time the Invader's swing finds contact with my blade.

"Impressive, hatchling."

Stop calling me that! I wish I could scream at him, but all I can do is respond with the Sword. I'm vaguely aware of the others around us, fighting off the remaining SSA companies, but my focus remains solely on the Invader. I can't stop myself, I have to take him out.

Neither of us has a real advantage, much like our last duel. It's becoming painfully obvious that we're too evenly matched, even as the remainder of the battle rages. I'd like to think I'd have an advantage if I had my other arm to use, but my right arm is virtually useless … I'm pretty sure the Invader broke it … so it dangles behind me. Every swing is parried, every thrust avoided.

A blast of magic energy strikes the Invader broadside, and I see Michi, hand thrust forward, her knees shaking slightly. I know she's overexerted herself again, so she's going to be weak.

Unfortunately, the Invader's figured that out as well. *"Another little bitch … haven't you learned yet, young lady? You can't win with a weak power like that!"*

The Invader turns to fully face Michi, Sabre at the ready. He rushes. Michi blasts, but this one's much weaker, and she collapses. I watch only for a moment more, as the Invader lifts his weapon high over his head, intent on sending the deathblow.

I rush toward him, Sword at the ready. My eyes don't deviate from my target: I watch as Fahaian distracts the Invader slightly, using his telepyretic abilities to ring the hell knight in a fire pillar. The Invader responds with a quick fist out of the flames, catching the prince across the face and knocking him out of the battle.

Michi is slightly less dazed, as she looks up from her kneeling position. The Invader raises the weapon again, completely over his head …

I have to do this …

My right hand grips the Sword. Pain jolts up my arm and across my chest. I'll only have one strike, tops. The Sword is raised over my head. My body screams, to make up for my mouth's inability to …

The Sword comes down in a hard, swift swing on the Sabre. I will probably never know the cause of this … if Fahaian's flames helped, or I found something, or if it was just plain fate … but upon the loud, explosive contact of the Sword, the Sabre shatters like glass.

The Invader lingers for only a moment before realizing what has happened.

*"No ... no ... how could t*his happen?" Scolar wails as the armor of the Invader literally falls off of his body. The general drops to his knees, still clutching to the useless hilt of the destroyed weapon. He breathes heavily, almost hyperventilating.

The blade of the Sword winds up underneath Scolar's chin. He drops what's left of his weapon, his hands quickly above his head. As this happens, Gabe and Aunt Kitty approach.

"Okay, Alanna, I think we're good here. Stand down."

The Guardswoman nods and sheathes the Sword, allowing the real me to come back out. My arm is killing me ... I don't know how much longer I can handle this pain, but I have to say something as Scolar collapses to the ground like a rag doll. "I don't think he's going to fight much."

Aunt Kitty crouches down next to Scolar ... Dad ... and looks intently at the face. "Damn, Gabe, I thought you were lying ... this really *is* Cole!"

"Of course, I don't lie," Gabe responds very matter-of-factly. "We should discuss this later, though, we've got several more companies of SSA troops coming." He turns to Fahaian and William, who's shrunk back down to his human form and is gnawing on a strip of moose jerky. "Gentlemen, if you would, please confiscate the General's car."

Chapter Five: Captive

February 11th

It feels really good to be back at the Ranch. The whole Ranch.

Shortly after we got back from the MRZ, Uncle Cyrus informed us that we'd be rejoining the refuge in the Yukon. Once everything was secured, including a new government-issue SUV we brought back with us, the spell brought us back. The folks at the refuge were very happy to see us, especially Grandmother and Julian.

We were happy too ... happy to be out of the New Empire, at least for now.

The last day of re-acclimation, though, has been rough. We placed Dad in a room of the Ranch house where he could be kept under guard, and have been trying to take care of him, but ... every time I see him, he simply lies in the bed, his eyes glassed over, his mouth hanging open. Almost like he's comatose without the Sabre.

I'm still holding out hope. This morning, my first order of business ... even before breakfast ... is to visit him. I have a short stool set up next to the bed, where I've been sitting every visit and watching over him. My arm's been in a cast for the last few days, since Michi and Uncle Cyrus have been too busy to do any healing. It doesn't matter right now, because all I'm focused on is my father.

Please wake up, Daddy ...

"Hi Dad ... if you're in there ... I have so many questions to ask you. I want so much to ask you how you learned to control the Guardsman, or what it was like when you and Mom were adventuring. I want to know if I'm doing it the right way."

My eyes remain locked on the man, lying motionless. The room grows eerily quiet. I can hear his breathing ...

Then I hear it, the first sign of hope. The muttering again. I hear it very quietly, what seems like a nervous tic.

"Ariel ..."

My heart jumps. "Dad, is that you?"

He inhales deeply. Exhale. Mutter. "Ariel ..."

I stroke his cheek gently. "Dad, Mom's not here ... the blueshirts have her. I need you back, Daddy ..." Emotion is overcoming me too quickly. I bury my face into his chest, weeping, pleading with him between sobs. "Please come back to me, Daddy ... I need you ... I love you ..."

Inhale. Exhale. Mutter. "Alanna ..."

The difference is immediate. I sit up, quickly wiping tears away from my cheeks. "Daddy?"

Inhale. Exhale. Mutter. "Alanna ..."

My heart is racing, and my own breathing is getting quicker and shorter. "Daddy, come on, you can do it ... please come back to me ..."

Inhale. Exhale. Mutter. "Help ..."

Wait ... that's even more different, that's a word, not a name. I keep listening.

Inhale. Exhale. Mutter. "Me ..."

I back away from the bed. It's a message.

"Alanna ... help ... me." It's a cry for help.

"GABE!" I scream into the corridor. Not only Gabe, but William, Grandmother, and Aunt Kitty rush in with him in response.

I tell them what happened, and immediately Gabe approaches the bed and looks into Dad's eyes. "Hmm ... you say it's between breaths?"

I nod frantically. "When he was Scolar, he kept muttering Mom's name. Julian says he did it all the time, not just around me."

The others look amongst themselves. Grandmother approaches the bed next to Gabe, giving a cursory look over Dad's prone body. "He doesn't seem to be too badly injured ... though those eyes ..."

45

Gabe puts a hand on Grandmother's shoulder. "You haven't seen this, I guarantee you. This explains a lot of things." He excuses himself from the room.

William senses my emotional mess and approaches me, pulls me into a hug. I have no choice but to hug back ... I need some response. "He's in there, William ... he's in there somewhere ... he needs me to help him ..."

William clutches me tighter. "Whatever he needs ... whatever you need, Alanna, you can count on me." He kisses the top of my head gently. I really appreciate the affection right now.

Gabe rushes back into the room, this time with Uncle Cyrus. At this point, Aunt Kitty shoos both of us out, to give them more room. William helpfully suggests we should get some breakfast. We go down the hall to the dining room.

Aunt Kitty's cooking is usually irresistible, but my stomach's making emotional somersaults right now, so I don't have much of an appetite. I settle on a bowl of cereal and make my way to the table where Michi, Fahaian, and Julian are sitting. Michi is the first one to say anything. "Yeesh, what happened? You're looking a little rough, Alanna."

I smirk. "Thanks a lot, Michi."

She grins and shrugs. "What are BFF's for? Seriously, though ..."

I sigh and scoop a spoonful of corn flakes into my mouth. "I think Dad's in there somewhere ... he recognized me and asked for help."

Julian raises an eyebrow. "That's a surprise."

I look over to the man, my grandfather. "I have you to thank for even being able to notice what he says, Julian. You told me last year, he muttered a name under his breath." I shiver and take a deep breath. "The name was Mom's ... it was your daughter's name."

It looks like Julian's about to cry. Michi pats the old man on his shoulder. "It's okay, buddy. We'll get him up and around and you'll get to finally meet your son-in-law, 'kay?"

Michi tends to have a contagious smile. Julian finally catches it, and it creeps across his face. I realize that this is the first time I've ever seen the man smile. "Let's remain hopeful, then. I want to meet him too, and get to know my daughter better."

Now I'm smiling, even as my cheeks are still wet with tears. William squeezes me slightly, and I keep eating my breakfast. We remain silent for a long time, until we notice Gabe approaching the table, with Uncle Cyrus and Grandmother in tow.

"Alanna, we need to talk."

I turn questioningly. "Is Dad okay?"

Gabe sighs. "Your dad's still alive … it's just …"

Uncle Cyrus pats Gabe on the arm. "Let me break it to her, Gabe." The agent nods, and Uncle Cyrus continues. "What Gabe's trying to say, Alanna, is that his body's alive, but his soul is missing … and he's asking you for help to get it back."

It's too much to ask. I don't know if I can even handle this.

The words chill my spine, and make my injured arm throb. "How can I help with that? What do you mean? It's insanity."

The others murmur questioningly between themselves. Gabe motions for quiet. "I know it sounds crazy, but that's the situation."

Michi looks very concerned, and she's got her hand on my shoulder. It's Fahaian, next to her, who finally asks, "How is this possible? A person's soul and their body should be inseparable other than by death."

Gabe sighs. "This is ordinarily true. However, there's certain things about Cole that make him susceptible to having his soul separated, mainly involving the Invader."

My throat tightens up at the mention of the hellish paladin. "You mean his soul was lost when he drew the Sabre?"

Gabe clears his throat, a little uncomfortably-sounding. *I have a feeling he's going to give me a half-truth again.* "Partly, Alanna. Partly his only battle with the Invader as the Guardsman, as well. I assume your parents gave you the story, right?"

I nod. "When they stopped the Invader at Four Corners, when they faced Abaddon, Dad was badly injured and Mom had to draw the Sword."

"Very good, Alanna, that's correct. As a result of the injury, which was inflicted by the Sabre, your father was partly corrupted by the weapon. When he drew it as his own, though, the corruption was complete, and his soul was taken from him." Gabe sips on the cup of coffee he's just been handed by Uncle Cyrus. "And someone *else* took over."

That much I understand. Scolar took control of a body without a soul, used the Sabre, and ran the SSA for the Regents. I have a feeling I know the answer, but I ask it anyway: "Where did Scolar come from, then?"

Gabe strokes his chin. "Not quite sure of that, actually. He seemed a bit weak to be a regular demon. When you destroyed the Sabre, there was no dust."

Aunt Kitty and Uncle Cyrus are surprised by this. Uncle Cyrus blurts, "none at all?"

Gabe shakes his head. Dust is always the result when a demon meets its end by the Sword. If there was none, then I'm now frightened that perhaps I didn't destroy Scolar after all, that maybe he's going to resurface and try to kill everyone here using Dad's body.

"What do we need to do, then?" William's question brings us back to the rest of the group. William and Julian are sporting very concerned expressions.

Gabe's face darkens. "We need to find Cole's soul. Thing is, I haven't a clue where it is." He catches a glimpse of my dirty look and adds, "I'm not being facetious here, Alanna, I *really* don't know. So I'm going to need your help."

I'm caught by surprise. "How?"

"I could use all of your help, actually. I have a feeling that Scolar's origins will have a clue as to where Cole is right now, so I need all of you to do some research and see if you can find out anything ... and I mean *anything* ... about Tyrelius Scolar. Agreed?"

We all nod and agree to do the work. To be honest, any job lately that doesn't involve peril to life and limb is a welcome change of pace. We finish breakfast and leave the dining room, all of us getting ready to search for Scolar.

February 15th

I take it back. I think I'd rather fight blueshirts, because this research is boring as hell.

For the most part, all of our searches have turned up only things we already knew about Scolar. He's a four-star general in the SSA. He served in the Army for 22 years. He was hand-chosen by the Regents to be the Chairman of the Joint Chiefs of Staff, in addition to his work as the blueshirts' field commander. He is also an old friend of Jennifer Regent's.

Considering that the man identified as Scolar is my unconscious father, lying in a bed in one of the Ranch guest rooms, all of this research is worthless because it's all false. New Empire propaganda, mostly, with nothing of real substance that will be of use to us.

Last night, it was Fahaian who suggested widening our focus to other places and times. What was it he said about the issue? "Souls are timeless, and can go anywhere and any time. It is possible that Scolar came from the past rather than the present." Those words got us started looking at histories.

I'm flipping through the sixth history book in the darkened dining room, nursing a cup of coffee I was able to get away from Gabe's voracious thirst for the stuff, when I hear heavy footsteps behind me. I'm pretty sure I know their source. "Couldn't sleep?"

William's voice rumbles as he chuckles. "There are too many thoughts racing in my head for me to sleep, Alanna. Mostly I worry for you ... and for your parents." He sits down next to me and takes my hand. It feels really, really good against mine.

I wrap his hand with my other hand ... I'm so glad I'm out of the cast, though it required drinking more of Uncle Cyrus's medical vomit punch ... and look into the man's face. His worry shows through. His brow furrows. The darkness in his eyes, which I noticed the first time we met last year, is back, though not nearly as deep as it was. His lips form a gentle frown.

"Are you all right, Alanna? I haven't seen you sleep for a couple of days."

I sigh and rub my eyes, sipping some coffee. "I haven't been able to. When I close my eyes, I see Dad being tortured ... or Mom being tortured ... basically torture of all sorts, and I feel powerless to stop it. So I figured the best option for me, at least right now, is to *not* sleep and put all my energy into this searching."

William sighs gently. "I understand this." He slides closer to me. "Has anyone told you yet how I came to the refuge in the first place?"

I squeeze his hand gently. "Not really, I assumed you were chased by the SSA, same as most of them."

He nods and smiles slightly. "It's a little bit more complex than that." His shoulders droop slightly. "We lived peacefully until about five years ago, keeping our existence hidden in Menominee, and trying to help our neighbors as best as we could. Especially after the formation of Lake Regent, the hunting became scarce, and more and more blueshirts started making regular patrols.

"One night, my mother awakened me and urged me to throw on clothes and leave the house. The SSA was coming for us, she told me. I pulled on one outfit, packed another in a backpack, and ran out the back door. Grandmother was there ... I suppose you probably know that she really *is* my grandmother."

I'd assumed as much, but I simply nod a confirmation.

"I heard gunfire, and roaring. When I looked back, my mother was bursting through the walls, facing the blueshirts as the wendigo. She had told me long ago that I had the blood of the wendigo warriors flowing through me, but I did not think anything of it until that night. I watched as the blueshirts' guns punched holes in my mother ... I watched her bleed to death, watched her die in front of me ... and I snapped.

"The wendigo came to me, once it had left my mother. I became the beast, and I fought back. The wendigo fed well that night."

I shudder, knowing exactly what it is that the wendigo feeds *on.* "So you and Grandmother got away, and came to the refuge."

William nods, and his voice is starting to quake. "When I sleep at night, when I close my eyes ... I see my mother's face. I watch her being murdered by the New Empire. Not the wendigo, mind you, it's my actual mother ..."

His face droops, and I see the tears welling up in his eyes. On impulse, I wrap my arms around his shoulders, and he wraps his around my waist. We hold the embrace for a long time, as William lets all of his grief out on my shoulder. After a while, I look up at him.

"I promise you, William ... I promise you, when we finish this, you'll never have that nightmare again. I won't allow it."

He sniffles and smiles slightly, his voice but a whisper. "How do you propose to do that?"

I smirk. "I'm the Guardsman, y'know. I'm sure defending against nightmares is part of the job requirements."

He laughs. Not a chuckle, a full-bodied laugh. The turnaround from despair to humor is enough for me to know that he's feeling better. He thanks me with a kiss.

I respond with a yawn. "I'm sorry, I guess I *am* kind of tired." I put a hand on his arm and look up at him gently. "Could I ask you a favor?"

He nods. "Anything, Alanna."

With my other hand, I stroke his cheek. "Stay with me tonight. Help make the visions stop." I press my cheek to his chest. "Please?"

William doesn't respond verbally. Instead, he picks me up and carries me back to my room, where he lays me in my bed. The covers are wrapped tightly around me, to comfort me against the chill of the evening. Shortly afterward, I feel a large, warm body wrapped around me, as William pulls me into the circle of his arms. His scent and his warmth do more to comfort me than any blanket can.

It strikes me just then, in the calm darkness of my room. There's something important I have to say. I snuggle closer into his embrace. "I love you, William."

He rumbles quietly, pulling me tighter into his arms. The warmth and comfort of my surroundings are too much to fight by keeping awake. My eyes close, and before I know it, I'm deeply asleep.

Chapter Six: Immortal Soul

February 16th

The armored army, several thousand in number, reaches across an entire line of battle, from end to end. They face down an opposing horde in a defensive posture. Bronze armor plates, large round shields, and several short swords stand at the ready, with pike men interspersed amongst the entire force. No horses, though: horses are reserved for officers, and this force has three, spread out amongst the troops.

A signal trumpet sounds. The charge begins. The infantrymen storm toward the defenders, swords and pikes and arrows finding purchase in the opposing force. The heat of battle rises, bringing with it men's shrieks; the clanging and clamoring of weapons against armor and shields; the stench of death. The field becomes an ocean of violent humanity, with no other purpose but causing harm and destruction. Curses fly in three languages in all directions.

An officer rides up on his horse, moving through his troops. They genuflect to his obvious high station. He rides faster. Another officer approaches, dismounted, walking alongside his horse. The mounted officer draws his sword and kicks his steed into a gallop.

The sword cleanly slices the dismounted officer's head off. The allied officer. The mounted officer leaps off of his ride and starts cutting a swath through the soldiers on his own side. This is too much for this army to handle: they buckle beneath themselves and fall to the enemy. The remaining officer is overwhelmed, pulled from his horse, and slain.

The surviving officer turns toward the defenders. He kneels before the opposing general, his scarred face showing his hopefulness in being allowed to remain alive. His eyes, murder still flashing in them, focus intently on the dismounting opposing general.

"Ave Caesar, dominus et princeps."

The general smiles, offering a hand to the genuflecting enemy. "Surge, ducem legionis."

The kneeling man takes the general's hand, thankful for the aid to his feet. Only when he turns his face toward his own vanquished army do I see the face I have been searching for.

Tyrelius Scolar.

I awaken with a shriek, sitting upright in the bed in a cold sweat, panting. *It's too real, it can't be a dream ...*

"Alanna?" I'm barely aware of William's voice cutting through my panic. He's still lying in the bed, on top of the covers that still cover my lap. His face looks very worried, as he reaches a hand out to mine, trying to comfort me.

I'm aware now that my heart is racing. I clutch my chest gently, looking back at my friend ... boyfriend, I guess now. "I had a dream ... nightmare, but not like the others ..."

I leap out of the bed, over William's prone body, which is now thoroughly wrapped up in the discarded blankets. I grab a robe and throw it over the clothes I fell asleep in, rushing out to the dining room. After extricating himself from the bedding, William rushes to catch up.

He yawns as he jogs along. "What is it? What kind of nightmare was it?"

I sigh gently. "I'm not sure, but it might help us in our search. It's something I hadn't thought of before. Come on, let's see if anyone else is up."

In the house proper I find out that everyone's up, since it's about nine in the morning. I'd be self-conscious about emerging from the hallway at the same time as William, but right now I don't care. I make a beeline for Gabe, Michi, and Fahaian, sitting at the opposite end of the dining room table.

"Rome. Roman Empire."

Fahaian looks confused. "What about it?"

I'm panting, and I need to catch my breath. If I don't, this is going to sound even worse. "We started trying to find Scolar in histories. Has anyone looked at the Roman Empire yet?"

Michi motions toward us to sit down, which we do. Gabe strokes his chin. "I see some logic in it. 'Tyrelius' is a bit of a Roman name. What makes you so sure about it?"

It's blurted out before I can think of being embarrassed. "I had a dream about it."

Michi groans. "I had a dream about a harem of bodybuilders, that isn't going to help with finding this jerk. How's your dream any different?"

I shake my head … Michi at heart tends to be a skeptic, even as she uses supernatural powers of her own. "Because I saw his face, and I heard his voice, and he was speaking to someone in Latin."

Gabe drops his hands, clutching his coffee mug. "Do you remember what was said?"

"I think so …" I wrack my brain for the pronunciation I "heard" in my dream. "Something like … well, Scolar said *'ave Caesar, dominus et princeps,'* and then the other guy he was talking to said *'surge, ducem legionis.'* Does that mean anything?"

Gabe mutters slightly.

"What do those phrases mean?" William insistently asks.

Gabe relents and leans back in his chair. "The first phrase means 'Hail Caesar, my lord and prince.' It was a common salutation for a conquered land's subjects to a native Roman citizen." His brow furrows further. "It's the other phrase that worries me, because it means 'arise, leader of the legion.' You're sure this is what was said?"

I nod furiously. "Absolutely."

Gabe looks toward a stack of books, close to where Fahaian is sitting. "Fahaian, could you pull the third book from the bottom out, please?"

The prince nods and slides the asked-for book out of the stack. He slides it over toward me.

"Alanna," Gabe intones, "take a look at the picture about halfway through that book … it's around page 755."

I get a brief glimpse at the title of the book: *Roman Campaigns of Note*. I open the book up to the page Gabe asked for. There's a picture of a battle, looking eerily similar to my dream. Lines of Romans pour down on much larger lines of other soldiers, dressed differently from their Roman counterparts.

"This is it, Gabe … this is the battle I saw in my dream."

Michi and William both look over my shoulders at the illustration. "Where would Scolar be in this mess?" Michi asks.

I point out one of the non-Roman soldiers, one on horseback. "One of these. He was an officer, one of only three present on horses."

I'm shuddering. *He's right there, in this illustration.*

"I think we might have found him, folks." Gabe stands up and comes behind the group of us huddled over the book. "This is an artist's illustration of a major battle Rome waged against Carthage, during Hannibal's march on Rome. It's one of many battles that took place around the defense of Rome, but this one in particular is noted for one thing."

My blood chills. I think I know the answer. "A general of Carthage switched sides."

Gabe pats my shoulder. "So you've read it, then?"

I shake my head furiously. "I saw it! In my dream, he led a charge, and then murdered the other officers and a big chunk of his own men before turning himself and his surviving forces over to the Roman general." I start panting again. "When I saw the traitor's face, it was Scolar's. Clear as day, right down to the scars."

Gabe nods, and then removes himself from the group, taking his coffee mug with him. Doubtless he's going somewhere else, because he doesn't want to get into a fight with me. I don't blame him, though, I'd be worried myself in his shoes.

"But what does this all mean?" Michi sounds very worried.

"I don't really know" is all I can tell her. "At least we know what his origins might be. Where we go from here is anyone's guess ..."

I trail off. I don't have any answers, any more than Gabe does. Fahaian motions for Michi to come with him, and they go out the back door, hand-in-hand. Despite my worried state of mind, it's still kind of cute to watch the two of them together.

"What should we do now, Alanna?" William asks.

I don't know what to do. I need some help. I need Dad.

Out of ideas, I finally decide we should go check in on Dad. When we get to his room, I'm very surprised to see Julian there already, seated next to the bed. He stands up when we enter.

"He's still lying there, just ... staring off in the distance."

I nod toward Julian, acknowledging what he said. "As long as nothing different's going on. Has he muttered anything?"

Julian walks over to where William and I stand. "The same muttering I always have heard from him, Alanna. You're right, when I heard it closer and listened ..."

I feel sorry for my grandfather. I hug him gently. "It's okay, we're trying our best to get him back. Go on and have some breakfast, you look like you could use it."

Julian smiles, and then looks up at William. "Incidentally, Ruth mentioned that you should come see her. She needs your help with some of the injured folks in the refuge."

William nods. "I'll be there in a little bit." Julian pats William on the shoulder as he exits the room. I'm only vaguely aware of this because my attention has shifted to Dad. His face remains as peaceful as it has been for the last week, just blank and devoid of any kind of emotion. His breathing is steady, slow, and deep, and he continues to mutter.

I've come here every day, hoping and praying that he'll say something else again, but since the day I heard his cry for help, all he's muttered is Mom's name, over and over.

Maybe today will be different.

I take Dad's hand in mine. "Daddy, it's Alanna again. I hope you're feeling okay in there … wherever you are …"

I need to be strong. I need to face this like an adult. My eyes feel too warm again.

"Daddy, we think we might know who's been holding your body hostage. Gabe's here, working on a way to find him … to find you …" I lay my head on Dad's chest. I can hear his heartbeat, almost equally as slow as his breathing. "If only you could tell us …"

Inhale. Exhale. Mutter. "Alanna …"

My face shoots up toward Dad's. "I'm here, Daddy, talk to me. Where are you?"

Inhale. Exhale. Mutter. "Fire …"

I frantically motion toward William, who gets a pad and paper from a nearby table and starts writing down what Dad mutters. I need to make sure I don't miss any of it. "Go on, Daddy …"

Inhale. Exhale. Mutter. "Ice …"

Now I'm thoroughly confused. He just seems to be saying random things now. William is dutifully writing the words down, though.

Inhale. Exhale. Mutter. "Sticks …"

I squeeze Dad's hand. "Daddy, what does this mean? Dad?"

Inhale. Exhale. Mutter. "Hell …"

A chill goes up my spine. My breathing is starting to get quicker.

Inhale. Exhale. Mutter. "Find me …"

I've forgotten that I don't want to cry, and the tears stream down my face. "Daddy, I'll help you, I promise." I reach up and kiss his forehead before walking out of the room with William.

Fire ... ice ... sticks ... Hell ... find me ... what does it mean?

My mind suddenly locks in on two mutterings.

Hell ... find me ...

I clutch William's arm. "I know where Dad is!"

February 18th

It took until yesterday for Gabe to extricate himself from wherever he was hiding after I told everyone about my dream. At first, I only told him what Dad had said. "It adds up, Gabe. Fire, ice, Hell ... it all sounds very underworld-ish."

Gabe's eyebrows went up about an inch. "Where do you propose we will find your father's soul?"

My face hardened. "He's in Hell, and he wants us to get him out."

The agent's face creased with a smile. "Smart girl."

The last day since that conversation has been a whirlwind, but we have all been debating between ourselves about where to go from here. The conversation's still going on in the living room as I enter, the first satisfying meal in days in my stomach.

"... what kind of strategy is possible?" Fahaian's voice sounds confused.

"I know of a guide who can get us where we need to be. From there, we'll need a guide inside," Gabe intones.

I sit down next to William, who instantly clutches my hand. "What's going on?" I ask.

Gabe turns his gaze toward me. "If your father's in Hell, we need to get down there and fish him out."

I dread what this means. "Can't we just … I don't know, hold a séance or something? How was he pulled down there in the first place? Isn't Hell for dead people?"

"Some, yes … most of it, to tell the truth, but there's some still-living souls there." Gabe turns his eyes toward the others in the group. "If we knew for sure the means, it would be easier to bring his soul back, but right now a direct approach is called for."

William clutches my hand tighter. "What exactly do you mean by 'direct' approach?"

The agent sighs. "We need to send someone down there, in person, to locate Cole and bring him back to the world of the living."

I don't think I can believe my ears. "You're serious, aren't you?"

Gabe purses his lips. "As serious as I get."

"That's crazy!" Michi yells. "Someone's gotta risk their ass and go to Hell … literally?"

"I wish it was easier, believe me. This is the only way, though."

Michi and Fahaian clutch closer to each other. I notice Grandmother approaching the group, an equally serious expression on her face. "Gabe, we have trouble. Another group of supernaturals just came to the door, and they're not looking good."

The entire group of us, prompted by Grandmother's warning, rush to the door. When we get there, the scene is horrifying. Eight supernaturals kneel on the ground outside the house, all of them missing body parts of some sort. All eight are bleeding profusely; a couple of them look like they won't last the night.

Teresa and Trent rush up, and I can hear Trent audibly gasp. "Gary?"

One of the injured supernaturals looks up at the name. "Trent? That you, buddy?" He coughs up blood, more than the amount he's losing through the hole where his left ear used to be.

Trent rushes out to Gary's side, trying to help him into the house. Grandmother's voice, terse but gentle, advises everyone where to take these victims in the house so that she can treat them. We all choose one each to help inside, and I let the others collect a soul to carry in before I come out to the last one, obviously the most grievously injured.

The youngest, as well. She can't be more than thirteen.

The girl shakes in my grasp, the one eye remaining looking up pleadingly at me. "A-a-are you … the Guardsman?"

Words come rushing back in my head. Gabe's words. The supernatural community needs an icon. *If it wasn't me, it would be Dad.* "I am, little one. Save your energy, you'll need it."

The girl has a piece of paper clutched in her hand. She lifts it weakly up to me. "They said … they said to give this to you … said to …"

I take the bloody note from the girl and keep going further into the house. I lay the girl down on a fresh bed, where she smiles up at me.

"I believe … in … you …" Her remaining eye closes. Her breathing ceases.

My breathing is coming more quickly. I clutch tighter to the note the girl handed to me. When I finally collect myself enough to look at it, I discover the New Empire sigil at the top of the stationery. My vision goes red with rage as I open the page and read the words, hastily scrawled in capital letters.

SHARPE:

SURRENDER THE GENERAL
OR YOU WILL ALL DIE.

It's in a feminine hand, that much is clear. I don't know if it really was written by Jennifer Regent or not. Right now, I don't care; they just used eight mortally-wounded supernaturals to send me a message.

The message is clear.

I storm out of the room, back into the hallway, and search for Gabe. The search doesn't take very long, as he's standing in the hallway outside one of the other rooms where other victims are being treated.

My voice becomes a growl as I shove the paper into Gabe's hands. "I'll go to Hell and bring Dad back myself. These bastards have to pay for this."

Chapter Seven: Bypass

February 20ᵗʰ

Gabe must think I'm insane. I know what I need to do, though.

I've spent the time since the eight supernatural victims came to the door preparing for a long trip. In that time, six more of them have died; the lone survivor is Trent's friend Gary. I've kept track of their progress on the side while preparing, but it's been far from the front of my mind.

I don't know exactly how long it's going to take to get to Hell, or how long it'll take in Hell to find Dad, but I'm not going unprepared. I'm in the middle of packing my eighth change of clothes when Michi comes into the room.

"Hey girl, what's up?"

She's trying to keep the mood light, I know, and I love her for it. I'm just too focused right now. "How do you pack when you're going to Hell?"

Michi shrugs. "I dunno, the last time I went to New Jersey I didn't stay long enough to sleep over."

I chuckle. "Nice." Okay, she managed to get a laugh out of me. I close up my backpack and sling it over my shoulder. "Are you sure you want to come along? You might want to stay here with your parents."

She puts a hand on my shoulder. "BFF to the end, Alanna. I'm sticking with you. Mom and Dad probably prefer it that way."

That's probably the truth. "Okay then. Are you ready?"

She nods and grins eagerly, clutching my hand and leading me out of the room. At that moment, though, it occurs to me that this might be the last time Michi drags me anywhere with her typical uncorked enthusiasm. I feel my heart flutter, and I squeeze her hand a little tighter.

She looks back at me. "Are you okay?"

I think a tear just fell. I wipe it away. "I'm good, it's just … I need to see Daddy one more time."

Michi nods and smiles. "I didn't think you'd want to forget that. Okay, I'll meet you out in the living room." She jogs down the hallway. I turn toward the door next to me in the hallway and open it gently.

Today, it's Fahaian and Grandmother standing watch over Dad. He still has that blank look on his face, the glassy eyes, the dead stare. His breathing is just as slow.

Grandmother approaches me slowly. "He's just like he's been, child."

Fahaian pulls out his lighter. "I'll be joining the group going with you, Alanna. Let me know when we're leaving."

I nod, and then impulsively hug both of them at once. "Thank you so much, for all you've done for me and for Dad." I release them both after a long embrace. "I'll be along in a few minutes, Fahaian. Go on ahead, Michi already has."

His face lights up at the mention of Michi's name. *You guys can't fool me, Michi.* He leaves the room. Grandmother squeezes my arm gently, and then leaves herself. I walk over to Dad's bedside, sitting down on my bench once again.

My hand is on his right away. It's warm, but it's lifeless … there's no energy trying to respond to my touch. I shiver when I consider the rough texture of his palm against the smooth skin of mine. I can barely stand to even look at him like this, but I must, I know it. I need to let him know that I'm here.

That I'm coming for him.

"Dad, it's me again." My voice is a choked whisper. Will I be able to get this out? "Daddy, I can't stay very long, the others are waiting for me. I just wanted … need to let you know … I got your message. I know where you are, and I'm coming to get you. I'm going to rescue you. I don't know what's going to happen to me … or to you … or to us

... but I know I have to try. I know that you wouldn't sit back if it were the other way around, if it was my soul in danger."

My forehead's on the back of his hand. I'm clutching his hand with both of mine now. "Daddy, I love you. I'll save you."

The room grows quieter. The rhythmic sound of his breathing is only interrupted by a quiet creak.

The creak makes words. "Alanna ... proud ..."

The floodgates open. I stand up and kiss him on the forehead. My tears are coating my cheeks; I wipe them off before leaving the room, even though I know they'll continue to fall. I look back before closing the door, trying to keep the image of Dad's face, burn it into my mind, so that I remember what my goal is.

Daddy, I'm coming for you.

I step into the hallway and continue into the living room. My friends are already there, waiting for me. Fahaian and Michi, holding hands like they've usually been doing since I've returned. Gabe and Uncle Cyrus, discussing some sort of plans laid out on the coffee table. Aunt Kitty, cleaning out one of her rifles, clearly anticipating trouble. Julian and Grandmother conversing by themselves. Finally, there's William, sitting on the couch across from Gabe and Uncle Cyrus, looking over the plans with them. He notices my entrance and stands up.

"I'm ready" is all I can say.

William sees my tears and pulls me into an embrace. "I'm with you, Alanna." I return the hug tightly before turning back to Gabe.

"Okay, let's go."

Gabe nods and smiles. "All right. Cyrus, if you please?"

Uncle Cyrus nods, motioning for us to approach the back door. The entire group of us follows his instructions, and once he's back at the front he leads us near his shed.

Only we're not going to the shed. He's leading us to the Avalon doorway. He places his hand on the knob of the nondescript wood door, only distinguished by being hung from a jamb that isn't built into a wall. His eyes close, and he focuses on his hand. The knob glows gently, a soft orange color.

"Everyone must go through quickly. I can only keep the portal open for a minute."

We all make sounds to acknowledge Uncle Cyrus's warning. With that, he turns the knob and the door opens toward us.

The scene on the other side of the door is an amazing paradise, lush and green, sunny and warm. Birds fly against a sky so blue it reminds me of my family's home in Arizona. I can hear creeks running, waterfalls flowing, and best of all, the sounds of living people. The others pour through the doorway ahead of me. Gabe, Aunt Kitty, Michi, Fahaian, Julian … all of them pass through in front of me. William motions and we head for the door, hand-in-hand. He steps through first, and I follow close behind.

Immediately, the weight on my heart is gone. It's replaced by the sheer joy of being in this paradise. I take a deep breath of Avalonian air, cleansing my lungs of the wintry cold. Behind me, I hear a soft click as Uncle Cyrus closes the doorway behind us. When he lets go of the knob, the door disappears.

Michi looks a little alarmed by this. "How will we know where the door is, Dad?"

Uncle Cyrus chuckles. "We don't have to. When we need to go back, Avalon will present it to us. We don't need it right now, so it's not going to hang around where it's not needed."

Aunt Kitty groans. Obviously, she doesn't think Uncle Cyrus should be having so much fun with this situation, although I can't really blame him.

I'd be happy if I could return home, too.

The others, though, are as awestruck by the sights and sensations of Avalon as I am. Fahaian rushes to the river, crouching and drinking handfuls. Julian simply stands in the meadow we have emerged into, taking deep, shaky breaths and gazing up into the sky. William picks me up in his arms and carries me over to a nearby tree.

"It's paradise, Alanna. I hadn't even thought to imagine this." William seems very much in awe.

"Neither did I, believe me." I stroke his cheek gently. "But I'm glad I could witness it with you, and all of my friends."

He smiles and looks over at me. His joy at the scene is tempered by fear, that much is clear. He's fearful about what I'm about to do, about the dangerous journey I'm about to undertake. I cling to him tightly.

I'm frightened, too.

February 21st?

It took an entire day for us to acclimate to Avalon's climate. It's too bad we have to leave it so soon; I'd really like to hang out here a little longer.

Some of the faces here are very familiar, since I met them last year at my birthday party or some beforehand. A very friendly face is Jerry Tile, who apparently hasn't spent much time settling in: he's still looking for a place to call home. The others have made him popular, though, since his supernatural ability comes in handy when they break their electronics: he simply has to hold the devices in his hands and they fix themselves.

I guess you never forget your first, even when it's your first rescue.

I've lost track of some of the group that came here with me, as I've spent most of the period here with William. We walk through the peaceful meadows that dot the Avalonian landscape, enjoying the weather and each other. Our talks have been made of few words and mostly out of enjoyment of our closeness. It's only now hitting me how much I really did miss William while I was in hiding … and he's certainly not shy about showing me how much he missed me.

This morning we were going to take a swim in the calm lake at the center of the land, but Gabe called us on some sort of urgent meeting. Slightly disappointed, we followed him, and now we're standing in a very lush area, staring up at a gigantic tree.

Gabe turns back toward us. "Kids, I need to talk to you, straight up. Have a seat." He motions toward the tree trunk. We sit down beneath the wide, leafy canopy, nearly obscured within the shadows cast by the leaves.

I'm the first of us to ask. "What's up?"

Gabe clears his throat. "I've made arrangements for you, Alanna, for your rescue mission. But you need to be prepared before you jump feet-first into Hell. So I've arranged this time to coach you." He reaches into the pocket of his coat and brings out a book. "First, here. You'll need this, and I want you to try to follow along as I talk, okay?"

I take the book from Gabe, looking at the cover. A hellish image is printed on it, a demon with its tongue sticking out, some kind of primitive representation of evil I guess. The title is printed directly below the devil image.

THE DIVINE COMEDY
PART I: INFERNO
Dante Alighieri

I'm confused now. "Follow along with this? I don't get it."

Gabe points toward the book. "That's the best guide you've got to what to expect when you get down there, Alanna. Keep that with you. It's your road map, so to speak. Make sure you've read it before you leave Avalon."

William pats my shoulder. "It's a decent read, Alanna, I've read it myself."

I sigh. I'm obviously outvoted on this. "Okay."

"Good, now follow along." Gabe walks away briefly, and then returns with a pad on an easel. A wedge-shaped drawing is scrawled across the pad. "Look at this carefully. This is the structure of Hell, according to Dante."

The map is intricately detailed, despite its rough look. Many names are on the drawing, names that seem otherworldly and familiar all at once. *Dis. Limbo. Ptolomaea.*

One name suddenly jumps out at me: *Styx.* "I think ..."

William nods. "Maybe that's what your father meant by 'sticks?'"

"Exactly," Gabe confirms. "This was why I was sure he was sending you a message of where to find him, Alanna." He pulls out a laser pointer. "Now, take a look. Hell is divided into nine Circles, each subsequent one lower than the previous one, until you reach the Center of Hell. Every level has its own dangers. Every level has a certain sin that it punishes. Some of them are subdivided further than others."

I focus on the bottom of the map, and find another familiar name: *Lucifer.* "So the Devil is at the center of Hell?"

Gabe nods. "Be very careful around him, Alanna. Never forget, he is the Lord of Lies. It will take all of your willpower to avoid falling prey to his charms."

I clutch to the Sword. "What about this?"

"I'm not exactly sure how the Sword's going to work down there. Theoretically, it may not even be allowed in ... it's a holy item being smuggled into an unholy place."

I snuggle closer to William. The thought of no Guardswoman is sickeningly terrifying right now.

"I'm not sending you down there without any defenses, either. I've spent the last few hours preparing something special." Gabe reaches behind the easel, and produces an oversize belt, from which hang three gallon-size milk jugs, all three marked with the sign of the Cross and filled to the brim with clear liquid.

I feel stupid for asking, but I do anyway. "Holy water?"

"Correct. Above all, Alanna, your journey is going to have to be a fast, out of necessity. There is no suitable food for you in Hell, and if you allow yourself to consume anything hellish in origin the consequences could be devastating. What this basically means is you'll have to *drink* this."

I swallow hard. "All three at once?"

Gabe rolls his eyes. "Of course not. Spread it out, but be careful. This is all of it you can have with you while you're down there. Consume it sparingly."

He hands me the belt. For carrying three gallons of water, it's surprisingly light. "Anything else I need to know?"

"As a matter of fact, yes. I've arranged two guides for you, one to get you to the gate and one to lead you *through* Hell. One other thing … there's the matter of time dilation to deal with."

Now William looks slightly upset. "Time dilation? What do you mean by that?"

Gabe sighs and clears his throat. "You're experiencing it right now, as a matter of fact. In a nutshell, time passes slower in non-Earth planes of existence than it does in the real world. You'll feel it like normal time, your body will act like the slower time is a regular day, but on Earth the time will pass faster. Included with those planes of existence is Avalon and Hell."

I raise an eyebrow. "How much dilation?"

"Well … I can tell you Avalon's, but I'm not entirely sure about Hell. One Avalonian day is equivalent to approximately a month and a half … about 45 days … in the real world. Hell might be longer or shorter, I'm not entirely sure."

Good grief … we're losing *that much time?* "What about the people we left at the Ranch, undefended?"

"They're in good hands, Alanna, don't worry." Gabe's reassurance sounds a little empty to me, but I have no choice but to accept it, really. "The point is, when you return to the real world it's going to be a lot later than you think."

I'm angry again, but I try to hold it back. I'm not angry with Gabe, really … it's more the situation that I'm mad at, that I have to deal with this, that I'm going to have to risk my neck and lose so much time in trying to get to Dad.

I stand up, the shadow of the tree still obscuring me. "When do we leave?"

Gabe smiles slightly. "I'll give you a day. This time tomorrow, everyone is to meet me over at the shore of the lake, which is how we're leaving."

Chapter Eight: Separation

April 3rd

I think I have this time dilation down. Even though Gabe believes the folks at the Ranch are safe, I still worry. Maybe it's just my nature to worry about people I care about.

Gabe's lesson was fairly short, simply a basic overview of what to expect in Hell and how to navigate. I hope the guides he's set up are going to know enough not to mistake me for a soul, though. What matters more to me right now, though, is that the lesson is over and this allows me and William to continue about our business, which in this case means our postponed swim in Avalon's crystal-clear lake.

We find it's really hard to get started with our plans. For starters, the lake is beautiful. Wildlife and plants ring it in a constant swath of natural beauty, enhanced just a touch by the natural magic of the place. The sunlight, forming into what's going to be a dazzling sunset, shimmers along the surface of the water, glowing and bathing us in its light. It's very hard to violate this stillness.

Another thing that's not helping is that right now we can't seem to let each other go. We've become very clingy … desperately so. It's hard to separate myself from William, from his warmth, his embrace, his scent. It's all very comforting, in a way that's hard to quantify.

I feel like I'm about to cry, just from how much I'll miss him. William notices this, and turns my face up to meet his.

What do you say to one of the most important people in your life before taking a trip into danger?

William finds the words for me. "Don't worry, Alanna. We'll be all right. While you're down there, you focus on your dad, focus on finding him and bringing him home."

I clutch tighter to William. "I'm scared."

He buries his face in my hair. "I am, too. Scared for you. Scared for everyone."

I reach a hand up to his cheek while turning my face up to see his. "If this succeeds, though … if I *can* find him, if I can get him out of there, then there's absolutely nothing we can't do. And that includes taking the country back."

It's always a little awkward to do because he's so tall, but I jump up, wrapping my arms around his shoulders, and bring my face up to his. "Thank you for believing in me … and for caring." The words are followed by a loving kiss. His arms tighten around my waist, and mine tighten around his shoulders.

This is the eternity I want.

I slide back down to the ground and smile up at him. "Come on, let's swim." I prevent any protest on his end by quickly stripping to my underwear and running into the clear lake, letting my wings out to help me stroke away from the shoreline. I hear a loud splash behind me, which tells me he's in the water as well, and slow down to allow him to catch up. When he does, we resume our embrace from on dry land, simply reveling in each other's company.

After a few minutes, though, I'm aware of us being watched. My eyes reluctantly tear away from William to scan the shore, only to find no one there. My glance shifts to the center of the lake, and that's when I'm startled by the appearance of the top of someone's head.

Only it's huge … and very feminine.

The eyes glow with a pale blue light. The flesh seems almost like water itself. Both of us splash away quickly from the figure as the head begins lifting itself out of the water, revealing a very large woman's head wearing a crown of ice, staring right at us.

She smiles and her mouth opens to speak. "Please, do not let me interrupt. Continue. "

I'm lucky not to have skittered back to the shore, collected my clothes, and gone running, but something about this woman tells me that's unnecessary. A response would probably be polite, though. "If it's all the same, we probably shouldn't. Are we disturbing you?"

She laughs and continues to rise out of the water. Once she's waist-high out of the water, it's difficult to stay in her presence just because of the appearance of her, this giant woman who would be about nine of William, formed from water apparently ...

... and also very obviously naked. William's blushing and doing his best to turn away from the sight. It's kind of cute, actually.

"I never mind this sort of disturbance. " She focuses her eyes on me. "You are Alanna Sharpe, am I right?"

I nod. "Please forgive us, this lake is just so perfect ..."

"Oh please, I have no trouble with you being here. If I did, you would certainly know. " She's laughing again, a very gentle chuckle. I realize she's laughing at William's desperate attempt to turn away. "You must be William White Bear. Please, there is no need for that. This is my only form of presence. Everyone else is used to it. "

William turns back around, and I can still clearly see his discomfort. Now I can't help but laugh. She's laughing too.

"I apologize, I am being rude. Here I know your names, and you know not mine. " The lady bows deeply, still smiling. "I am known by many names throughout history, but you may know me as the Lady. "

Okay, a giant lady ... is standing in a lake. Way too Arthurian, but then again I'm in Avalon, so what did I expect? "How do you know us?"

"Gabe asked me to come fetch you, but before then I knew of you. You see, you know my son. " The Lady motions to the shoreline. We turn around to notice that a familiar figure is appearing in the dying light of the afternoon.

Uncle Cyrus waves to us. "Alanna! William! We're getting dinner in a second."

The Lady melts into the lake quickly. In a flash, a smaller version of her is rising up along the shore, embracing Uncle Cyrus. William leads the way as we swim back over, arising on the shore and reclaiming our clothes.

Uncle Cyrus releases the hug the Lady is giving him. "I see you guys met Mom." He smiles widely. As we stand and watch, it looks like he's actually growing a little bit. "She's going to help you tomorrow when you leave, Alanna, so Gabe figured you should get used to her."

The Lady turns to me and smiles like Uncle Cyrus ... I see where he got his face from. At the normal size of a human being, the Lady has a very slender build, ageless face, and not a single sign of imperfection. She's the perfect woman, rendered as an ice sculpture. "I live through the waterways around the world, so most entrances and exits from this place pass through me."

I think I can handle that, at least. "Will you be coming to dinner?"

She sighs with a slightly wan expression on her face, and that's when I notice that her body is incomplete, and one leg is still in the water. "Sadly, I may only be present in Avalon's bodies of water. Were I to go up on land, I would surely perish, and with me would die Avalon."

That makes me sad for some reason. "I understand. We'll be ready in the morning."

She smiles and retreats back into the lake, melting into the shimmering sunset reflection. I'm just pulling my shirt back on when I hear William's question. "The Lady of the Lake is your mom?"

Uncle Cyrus nods. "Deep secret. Don't let anyone else know about it, I just want the others to think of me as a regular guy."

I smirk. "Not sure that's possible. Are we going to find out your dad's Merlin, too?'

"Now that you mention it ..."

Our laughter kills this conversation, as we make our way to where the others wait for us, the steaming aromas of Aunt Kitty's cooking beckoning us closer.

May 20th

Last night was tough. The dinner was wonderful, as I've come to expect from Aunt Kitty's cooking, but it was just the raw emotions that made it difficult.

My friends are all worried about me, worried that I won't return from this mission. Not that I can blame them, but I'd really appreciate some positive thinking, especially from those who are closest to me. I sit here now, as the sunrise is barely above the horizon, and look at these friends I'll be leaving behind, and it only makes this task that much more difficult.

Michi was a wreck. It made me just as bad, since we're more like sisters than best friends, but I have to be strong for her. She lies next to the barely glowing embers of our magical fire, huddled close to Fahaian, who has an arm lightly draped over her in slumber. Although I'm slightly jealous that Fahaian has her attention, I'm really happy for the two of them. I want them to be happy, to be together.

Not far from those two, I spot Uncle Cyrus and Aunt Kitty, in much the same position. I put a cheek idly on my hand as I observe my sleeping friends.

Two couples, born to be together.

The reverie brings my attention to William, curled up next to me. He's still asleep, his face showing more peace than he ever shows when he's awake. His hand reaches idly for my hip, as he's obviously dreaming. I pick up his hand slowly and bring it to my lips, this strong hand of a man who I've come to love dearly, even more than I could have ever imagined.

Last night, he insisted on accompanying me to the entry point of Hell. I'm glad for this. *I'll need his strength to walk through the gate.*

There's hours to go before we're to meet Gabe at the lake, so I decide to take some exercise. I stand up, stretch my back, and unfurl my wings. Gently, so that I don't disturb the others, I walk out of our little circle, flap my wings, and take to the air.

The atmosphere of Avalon embraces me like a loving parent. The air is crisp and clear, the weather perfect, as very few clouds are crossing through the newborn sunlight. I flap my wings to drive myself higher. The sky seems so infinite when I'm up this high, calling to me, beckoning me to fly even higher, to touch the sun. The temptation of Icarus overcomes me, and I reach out to the bright orb in the sky.

"Are you sure you want to do that?"

A voice? This high up? I heard that, it wasn't in my brain. Who could be up here?

"Others before you have tried to touch the sun, with bad things happening for their effort."

I need to know who this is. The voice sounds like it's behind me, so I turn in a gentle corkscrew. I finally spot the speaker, an older man with large, feathery wings spread behind him, flapping in pace with my own. I raise an eyebrow. "Am I to assume you've tried before?"

"Every once in a while. I like to challenge myself." He smiles playfully. "I heard you were here, and I had to come see you. Let's talk on the ground."

I'd agree to that … a conversation's a little difficult to conduct while flying. I follow my elderly companion to an unoccupied meadow, where we alight and land in sync. My wings curl up into my body; his, though, remain behind him, folded like a bird's wings. He's approaching me now, with his hand extended in a friendly gesture.

"Hi, pleasure to meet you, I'm Carlos del Aire. I've been here a few days." He extends his hand to me. "I've wanted to meet you since I heard about your actions in Chicago."

I can feel my face reddening ... I really didn't want a reminder of last year. "Thanks ... I guess?" I shake his hand firmly. "Right now, I just want to stretch my wings, get some peace ..."

Carlos narrows his eyes playfully. "You're avoiding things, Ms. Sharpe."

I wrap my arms around myself. "Avoiding what? Nobody else volunteered to go into Hell. Nobody else was pushing me aside to rescue Dad."

He smiles and raises a finger. "Ah yes, you have stepped forward for this ... but now that you have, you don't want to go."

Am I *that* transparent? My heart aches right now. "Yeah ... I guess that sounds right. I'm starting to realize what it is I've chosen to do, I guess. It's starting to feel like it's too much for me."

Carlos looks playfully confused ... does this man take anything seriously? "But if it's too much, why choose to do it?"

I sigh. "It's my duty. I'm the Guardsman, it's up to me to do this. No one else needs to take the risk, only me. It's my family, after all."

"Yes, but ..."

"Is that all you say, things that start with either 'yes' or 'but?'"

He chuckles. "Not always. Sometimes I start sentences with 'you.' As in, you need to realize that others see your father as family, as well. As well as you yourself."

That's the truth ... why else would they have come for me at Traverse City last year? Michi said I needed to figure out that they love me. I think I know that, but it's only just now starting to sink in, only now that I'm about to dive into the most dangerous adventure of my life.

Tears are starting to fall, and Carlos realizes this. He places a hand … and a wing … on my shoulder. "Your friends care, Alanna, just as much as you do. It's your duty, yes, but you also need to come to terms with your feelings for them, and their feelings for you. Remember who you do this for."

I sniffle and look up at the old man, feeling his feathers tickling my shoulder. "Dad? Mom?"

"Them too, yes, but you also do it for your friends. You do this for *everyone* you love."

My smile comes gently, as what he's said sinks in. I do this for everyone. Not just myself, not just for my family, but for everyone. My voice is soft. "Are you an angel, Carlos?"

He laughs. "Oh my no, Alanna, I'm merely an old man from New Mexico. Real angels are far more subtle than me …" His eyes rise away from me. I follow where their gaze points and find Gabe, approaching slowly. I slide out gently from under Carlos's wing and approach the agent.

"Everyone's wondering where you are, Alanna." He turns his eyes up. "Carlos, I'm sorry about this."

"Not at all, Mr. Francis, we've been having a good discussion." He turns toward me. "Remember what we talked about when you go down, young lady."

I smile wider now. "Don't worry, I will. Thank you." Gabe puts his arm around my shoulders and leads me away as Carlos flaps his wings and takes to the air once more.

"Interesting discussion?" Gabe sounds nosy, but I know he only cares.

"Quite. I think I'm ready to go."

He smiles. "Smart girl."

Gabe leads me back to the campsite, where everyone else is awake now. He has a hand on my shoulder as we approach, and he raises his voice to gain everyone's attention.

"Folks, this is it. Where we're going now very few have ventured before, but not all of you can come with us." He squeezes my shoulder as William comes to my other side. "Alanna, it's time."

There's a small creek bend near the campsite, and as Gabe speaks I watch the Lady rise out of the water, shimmering in the light of the day. I take a deep breath.

This is it.

My farewell path starts with Uncle Cyrus and Aunt Kitty. "I want you guys to know, you've been wonderful to me since I came to be at the Ranch last year. I'm so glad to have you in my life."

They both hug me, Aunt Kitty at my shoulders and Uncle Cyrus at my waist. I think Aunt Kitty might actually be crying … I've never seen her cry before. When she speaks, her voice shakes. "You stay safe down there, girl, and find your dad."

My heart is throbbing. This might be too much emotion, but once the Salems have let me go, I move over to where Julian stands, smiling weakly. His voice is quiet this morning. "Does it have to be you?"

I take a resigned deep breath and nod. "Absolutely, Julian. He called to me, and …" I wipe a tear away from my eye. "… and I'm the only one who can find him, who can save him."

He nods, and then wraps his thin arms around me, pulling me tightly to him. "Find him, Alanna. Bring him home, so we can get my daughter back."

I hug my grandfather as tight as I feel safe doing, clutching to his shirt shakily. "I will, Grandfather."

He's surrendering to emotion himself. I release him and gently kiss his cheek, then move over to the last ones I have to see before we leave, Fahaian and Michi. The prince extends his hand to me. "Good luck in your quest, Alanna.

May Aten and Zoroaster smile on you as you journey into peril."

I'm not satisfied with a handshake. Instead, I embrace Fahaian, if only to give him a quietly whispered message. "Be courageous, and take care of Michi. She's going to need you."

He whispers back, "I will."

I release Fahaian and turn to Michi, who I've purposely saved for last. She looks inconsolable … I think she's been crying the whole time. I playfully poke her shoulder. "Don't be such a baby, Michi … you'd think you were going to school or something."

I wink at her. She giggles gently, though she's still emotional. "Come home soon, okay? We'll keep your room open for you." Even though I know it's coming, it still knocks me off-balance when she glomps me. "You take care and find your dad. We'll be okay."

Now my tears are falling. I clutch her tightly. "Michi, if it comes down to it … remember that you're the best friend any girl could ever have."

After what feels like a sad eternity in each other's arms, I feel the gentle pressure of William's hand on my shoulder, signaling that it's time to go. I release Michi from my grip and back away from the group.

Something doesn't feel right here. I need to say something.

I clear my throat, but my voice is still a little bit of a hoarse croak. "Hold strong for me while I'm gone. Resist. Fight them to the end. This isn't over until the New Empire's gone."

I hold my hand up to wave at them. They return the wave, and at this point I need to turn away from them and approach the Lady, with Gabe and William flanking me. A shadow passes over us, and I look up to see Carlos del Aire flying overhead.

An air tribute.

I can't help but smile now. My attention is now focused on the Lady, who stands with her arms open, kind of expectantly. "It is time, my friends. Step into the water."

The three of us approach the Lady, stepping gently into the creek bend. The water penetrates my shoes, but it feels right for some reason, probably because of the Lady's influence. We continue to wade until we're all waist-deep in the creek bend.

The Lady raises her arms. "I can only take you as far as the waters will allow. You will be on your own to reach your destination once you leave my world."

"I understand," I reply. "Let's go."

The Lady smiles at me, even as her arms cease their human appearance and take on the form of a crashing wave, approaching us. Engulfing us. Still, the water doesn't feel wrong, even though I should fear drowning. It feels more like comfort … like an unexplainable state of relaxation that washes over me.

Like floating in the womb.

Chapter Nine: Goddesses

May 20th, continued

I'm aware of my two male companions. None of us can talk, since we're all surrounded by water. Gabe is stoic as ever, but William appears to be panicking. I reach an arm through the coursing liquid to stroke his cheek, to reassure him. In the distorted light of the wall of water I see him ... then feel him ... clutch my hand in his own and press it closer. His features instantly relax at the touch.

I don't know how much time has passed, but I can sense the waters thinning. Earth comes up underneath our feet. The waters start to recede from above our heads as we stand on the new ground, but my hand hasn't left William's cheek. I feel the dryness of the air as the water continues to recede, until we emerge ...

... on a beach covered in black sand. I'm unsure if we have reached our destination, but Gabe seems sure of it. William returns my hand to my side. I want to speak, but I'm afraid to, still afraid I'll drown. As it is, I feel slightly waterlogged as I take a deep breath.

"My friends, you have arrived. This is as far as I can take you. You must walk from here. " The Lady reaches a hand out to me, which I take gently and feel the dampness that's her nature. She suddenly pulls me into a soggy embrace and kisses me on the forehead. "Good fortune and good voyage to you, Alanna Sharpe. Save our world. "

"Save our world?" What does *that* mean? I gather myself and return to the sandy shore, taking William's hand in mine, as the Lady recedes into what I'm guessing by the smell is the ocean. My attention is immediately on Gabe. "Where are we?"

He seems to be looking around away from where the waves are crashing against the beach. "If I'm not mistaken, we should be in Hawaii."

Okay, it looks suitably tropical. That would explain the black sand, too, if we're on an island with volcanoes ...

Oh my God, is that how I'm going to get to Hell?

William gets Gabe's attention before I can vocalize my thoughts. "What are you looking for?"

Gabe smirks. "Not what exactly, but 'who.'" He raises his hands to his mouth. "Hi'iaka! Come out!"

Rustling comes from high up on the shoreline. Very loud rustling, and it mostly disturbs a big patch of ferns, next to a pair of very large rocks. We keep our eyes on the ferns, which eventually start moving in a patch toward us.

Okay, plants that move on their own. Nothing out of the ordinary there.

The patch of ferns slithers over to where we stand, just in front of us. Before any of us are truly aware of what's happening, they fly up, revealing underneath them that they are actually someone's hair. The woman who stands before us now looks almost my age, maybe a little younger. She kind of reminds me of Michi, actually, but her features and skin tone are decidedly Polynesian. The tanned body is wrapped in more of the ferns, which form a bra and a skirt for her, giving her the appearance of a hula dancer.

"Gabe Francis, wat da big idea? I'm undah covah here, brah!" The speech coming out of this woman doesn't seem to match the body.

Gabe seems unfazed, though. "We need to see Madam Pele, Hi'iaka. I know you can take us to her."

She harrumphs and crosses her arms. "All da time, you *haoles* come trampin' on da beach, messin' up da environment, makin' da place a mess, and whose *okole* gets reamed for it? Mine, dat's who! How you figgah I should take you guys see Big Sis Pele?"

"It's an urgent matter. It affects you and her as well."

The scowl that's crossed Hi'iaka's face softens slightly. "Who da *wahine,* Gabe?"

Gabe motions me forward. "This is Alanna Sharpe, the Guardsman of this generation. That's William White Bear, the latest wendigo warrior. We need Madam Pele to take us to the gateway."

"No way!" She approaches me and scans me too tightly. "Guardsman, huh? Now what do da Guardsman need wit' da door to da Inferno?"

My chest tightens. "Gabe, the door's *here?*"

"Not exactly, it's a little lower, but we need Hi'iaka's sister to take you there." He turns back to our confronter. "Now please, we have very little time and a lot to discuss. Please take us to Madam Pele."

Hi'iaka reaches for the Sword, but recoils slightly before she touches it. She shrugs finally. "Okay. Dis way, folks, an' try keep up, I walk fast." As the words leave her mouth, she sinks back down into the sand as quickly as she rose out of it, leaving only the ferns on the surface, and slithers further away from the shoreline. With one questioning glance between us, we all quickly jog behind the plants to keep up.

Hi'iaka's route takes us through some dense tropical forests, then into a field covered with the types of ferns that make up her hair and clothing. Every once in a while, so that we don't lose her, she pops her head up so that we can find which ferns belong to her specifically; once we see her head, we can watch the rustling of that particular patch and keep following. This continues for two hours, until we finally reach the entrance of a dormant lava tube, forming a deep cave in the island's forest.

The goddess motions into the tube. "Right dis way, folks. When you get to da end of da tunnel, hang a left and keep walkin' until you hit da uddah side of da caldera. You can't miss it."

Gabe nods. "Thank you, young goddess." He walks into the tube, leading the group of us. William is immediately behind Gabe, and then I follow.

To my surprise, Hi'iaka actually comes up behind me and follows us into the darkness. I look back at her briefly. "I didn't think you were coming with us."

"You gonna need somebody talk to Big Sis Pele for you, and it bettah be somebody Big Sis Pele trusts. She got a history wit' Gabe that ain't too cool."

Why am I not surprised? "Okay, stick with us."

We continue down into the ominous lava tube. In the middle, we encounter a wide puddle where rainwater's collected. We get dunked about mid-calf deep into the water, but we continue moving forward, feeling our shoes squish as we continue. Hi'iaka has no such trouble, since she's barefoot, which tells me that she's definitely a goddess since she's not complaining at all about the volcanic floor of this tube.

I'm certainly glad I'm not claustrophobic, since as we continue deeper into the tube, the walls start to get closer together. We reach the end of the tube together; there's not another branch off.

"How do we hang a left?" I ask.

"Feel on da wall. You'll find it."

Gabe taps the wall gently with the palm of his hand. We can't quite see him, but eventually I hear a crack, followed by his voice. "Got it. Through here." I hear an impact, followed by shattering. A piece of the wall flies toward me, taps against my chest, and falls into my hand. It's sharp, almost like glass.

Gabe turns back toward us. "It looks really tight through here, so we're probably going to have to crawl. You ready?"

William looks at me. "You can do this."

I smile back. "So can you." I turn behind me to look for Hi'iaka, only to see that she's dropped back down into the ground, with only her ferny hair sticking up giving us any idea that she's still with the group. Gabe has already started crawling through the branch. William climbs in behind him, and once I see the ferns start travelling, I finally climb in.

I'm going to be amazed if William gets through. It's hot, it's tight, and every once in a while I scrape my butt on the ceiling of the tube. There's no indication we're even making forward progress ... at times it gets pitch black and we can't see anything.

Then the glow starts. The hot, ominous glow of volcanic power surrounds us. I can see dark shapes ahead of me that can only be Gabe and William. I'm sweating so much that I think my clothes are saturated.

Better get used to it ... I'm going someplace even hotter.

"We're almost there, guys. I feel fresh air." Gabe calls back to us, but even his voice sounds a little rough. I'm panting from the heat. How are we going to even survive getting to the entrance?

One shape in front of me disappears. The end of the tunnel is close! I can feel a breeze ... I've never been so happy to feel wind on my face.

The giant shape that I know is William drops. I can see the end, see the light, the glow that's not coming directly from the rocks I'm crawling through. The air feels fresher, but still smells like sulfur.

"Hurry up! Big Sis Pele ain't got all day!" Hi'iaka's admonition spurs me forward. My head clears the tunnel, and the rest of me staggers through. Immediately, William's hands are wrapped around my arms to help me to my feet. I lean into his body, thankful that we've both made it, and only when I feel his head on mine do I look around.

We're in another volcanic chamber, this one illuminated from a central cone. The heat is not as bad here as it was in the tunnel, but it's still a little oppressive; I'm sure I'm not going to stop sweating anytime soon. Strangely, though, the rest of the room is sparsely furnished, with small tables and mats. There's no other door we can see, though, other than the tunnel we came through.

Hi'iaka seems unfazed. "Big Sis Pele! We got company!" She addresses her yell to the center of the room, which starts shaking immediately afterward. I clutch to William, but Gabe looks like he's done this before.

A shape rises out of the cone in the floor, much like the Lady emerged from the lake in Avalon. This shape is also female, but it's human-sized and composed of fire. It's in fact another beautiful woman in a regal-looking ankle length gown; a dress that almost looks ancient Greek except the material's much rougher than cotton. She stands before us, dark-skinned, dark-haired, and radiant, and steps down from the cone to face Gabe.

"I see. Hi'iakaikapoliopele, did I not tell you this man is not allowed in my home?" The woman's language is much more formal than Hi'iaka's, and what's up with that long tongue-twister of a name she used?

"I'm sorry, Big Sis Pele, dese mortals need get to da gate of da Inferno."

So this is Pele, this regal woman. Her eyes glow red, with anger … or annoyance … or some sort of negative emotion. Her mouth parts to show her gritted teeth. "How dare you, sister. You have been told no mortals may enter my presence. You know what happens."

Hi'iaka is cringing. "I'm sorry! I know, I'm sorry, please don't punish me …"

Pele points at the tunnel. "Go, sister. Go. Leave me. And this time, when I ask you to keep watch, actually *do* what I tell you to do!"

The goddess has kept her voice controlled, but the bitter rage virtually boils behind the words. Hi'iaka drops her head and shuffles slowly over to where me and William stand, near the tunnel. She places a hand on my shoulder. *"Aloha* and good luck, Guardsman."

Pele's ears perk up when she hears Hi'iaka's farewell. She turns around to face us for the first time, as Hi'iaka drops into the earth again, her ferns scurrying into the tunnel once more. Pele approaches us, narrowing her eyes.

"Did she just say you are a Guardsman?" She looks at William. "You don't look like a Sharpe."

"He's not. I am." My heart's in my throat, but I have to say something. I clutch the Sword tighter to me. Pele finally turns her gaze to me, and it chills me as her eyes, glowing with otherworldly fire, seem to pierce right through my soul. Surrounded by a nearly perfect face, the clear appearance of supernatural royalty, Pele scrutinizes me.

"Yes … yes, I see it. What is your name, child?"

I take a deep, nervous breath. "Alanna Sharpe." I bow my head slightly … is that the right thing to do? "I am the Guardsman, as my father was before me."

Pele chuckles. "You know, I was just talking about you … I didn't think I'd have the chance to actually meet you."

This catches me aback. "Talking about me? With whom?"

I hear laughing coming from the shadows … cheerful laughter. "With me, Alanna."

That voice ... My heart jumps with the familiarity. I hear her footsteps, and soon from a shadow emerges someone I've missed for a long time.

"Durga!" I rush up to the Hindu goddess and hug her, an embrace she returns with four arms. She's still laughing even as we're reunited. "I haven't seen you for so long, where have you been?"

She releases the hug gently to look me in my eyes. "I've been traveling around in supernatural circles, warning about the New Empire. Marshaling forces for you, you know."

I smile for the first time here. After last year, after storming off from my responsibility out of my anger with Gabe, I was so afraid she had abandoned me, but now I know she's been helping me the whole time.

Gabe and William approach Durga as well. "We're happy to see you," Gabe intones, "but why are you here? Did you know we were coming?"

Durga simply smiles. "Pele is a close friend of mine. Us warrior goddesses need to stick together, after all."

"Speak for yourself," Pele chirps with the slightest hint of a laugh. "I'm no warrior."

Durga chuckles. "I would not call your situation a temper problem, Pele. You're a warrior, you just do not realize it. I know a warrior when I see one."

Pele punches Durga playfully on her shoulder. Gabe finally clears his throat. "Ladies, while this is all well and good we have a mission that we're on and we need Madam Pele's help."

Pele nods. "So my sister has told me, you need to get to the door of the Inferno." She turns toward Durga. "Is everything you've told me about this girl to be believed, my friend?"

"That and more, Pele. As long as she maintains control over her powers and herself, there's no reason why she can't handle anything thrown at her."

Pele strokes her chin thoughtfully, turning her gaze toward me. "Come to me, child."

I slowly approach the goddesses, clutching the Sword tighter to my hip. This close to her, I can feel that Pele emits immense heat from all over her body, almost like standing next to the heart of a volcano. Which I suppose is pretty close to the truth, since realistically she *is* the heart of this volcano.

"Such strength … such power, I can feel it in you, child." Pele's face comes uncomfortably close, scrutinizing every hair, every line, every single little thing about me. "Show it to me."

Pele reaches a hand out and touches my cheek. Without thinking, my wings unfurl and spring out of my back. This seems to catch Pele by surprise as well, and she steps back slightly.

"Ah, I see, dragon wings." She turns to Durga. "I wasn't sure if I believed you about those."

Durga smirks. "Would I lie about something like that? She is the real thing, Pele."

Pele nods. "Are you the one wishing to cross into the Inferno?"

I take a deep breath. "I am. There's someone there I need to find and rescue … someone that I love, someone dear to me. He doesn't deserve punishment, yet he's trapped there, and I need to get him out."

Pele reaches out and lifts one of my wings, shaking it gently. "Seems sturdy enough, I guess. How well do these work?"

"I'd say very well." I puff my chest out slightly. Maybe I shouldn't be so vain, but I'm *proud* of my dragon nature and don't see a reason why I shouldn't be.

Pele nods. "Very well, then. I'll take you there. Steel your soul, child, because the journey is going to test your spiritual mettle." She motions to the room we're standing in. "Stay the night with me, all of you. In the morning, I will take you."

Chapter Ten: Downward

May 21ˢᵗ

Sleep was difficult to come by last night, but it finally came. Exhaustion overcame my anxiety.

The mats Pele offered us for the night are surprisingly comfortable, considering they're laid out on a volcanic rock floor. We've been spread to several different corners of the room, with Gabe directly across from me, on the other side of the glowing cone in the center. Despite the gentle glow, the cone hasn't been intrusive in terms of sleep.

I feel gentle breathing on my shoulder, and only then do I remember that William is with me, on my mat. He has an arm lightly draped across my waist, but when I turn to see his face his eyes are open, red, and watering.

"Are you okay?" I accompany my question with a gentle stroke of his cheek.

"Yeah … but …" His face droops, and I see the darkness returning to his eyes. "Alanna, I worry about you. I wish I could be with you, to protect you …"

Before he can blurt out any more, my lips are on his and I take my sweet time in removing them. "It'll be all right, William. It's really going to be okay. Before you know it, I'll be back with Dad."

William doesn't seem consoled. He clutches me tighter. "Promise me, Alanna."

My arms naturally wrap around his arms. "What should I promise you?"

His hand strokes my hair gently. "Promise me that you'll make it. Promise me that you'll emerge from there in one piece. Promise me you'll be alive." He buries his head in my shoulder. "Promise me that you won't forget about me, that you'll stay safe, and that you'll come back."

He's shuddering, and I can feel his tears. I run my fingers through his hair gently to console him. Even as we lay here,

I can feel my own tears starting as he weeps. I bring my lips to his ear, to whisper my response.

"I promise."

We lay clutched together for a long time, what feels like hours. It's finally up to Gabe to bring us back to reality, shaking my shoulder. "I hate to break this up, but we need to go. Pele is waiting for us."

I turn up my face toward Gabe and wipe some of my own tears away. "Okay, Gabe, thank you." I shake William gently to rouse him. "Come on, handsome."

Pele and Durga await us with a small meal, mostly bread and fish. As we eat, we spend time talking amongst ourselves. I fill in the gaps Durga left in her stories about me, some of which make Pele laugh, while others arouse her rage. The conversations blend into each other eventually, as my mind can't process them all.

My last meal ...

The feeling of being condemned is starting to overwhelm me. William seems to sense this, and wraps his arm around my shoulders. This gains Pele's attention. "Is he your lover, child?"

The question stops me short, mainly because I've never heard it put quite that way. "He's my boyfriend, yes." I take William's free hand in mine.

Pele turns her attention toward William. "Are you prepared to shoulder the burdens she brings back with her from the Inferno?"

I can feel him start to panic. "What do you mean?"

"Those mortals who venture into the Inferno find themselves changed by it. Some for the good, some for the bad, but no matter which there's a change. Those who have taken past ventures found their relationships severely limited once they emerged. Are you prepared for this to happen?"

He looks at me longingly and squeezes my shoulder once more. "I know the risks, Madam Pele, but I also know that this is the right thing for Alanna to do. I'm with her all the way, as far as I can go."

I snuggle closer into the man. Pele nods and smiles. "Such loyalty is admirable. Be warned, though, the changes that take place may test this. Don't be discouraged, just be warned." She stands up finally. "It is time, child. We must go."

The rest of us join her in standing up. Durga comes over to me. "I must continue to find our supernatural brethren and warn them. You're in good hands with Pele here." She hugs me once more. "Good luck, Alanna, but you'll do well. I believe in you." With those words, she melts into the shadows cast by Pele's conical light.

We're now all on our feet, surrounding our hostess. Pele crosses her arms. "I can take you men only so far. Once we reach the edge of the crater, only Alanna may come with me."

Crater? This is sounding worse and worse all the time.

There's not much we can say to dispute the goddess, so we all nod in agreement. Pele's eyes start glowing orange again, much like they were when she was raging at Hi'iaka, but this time she turns toward the wall she stands near. She raises her hands, and a door-shaped segment of the volcanic rock face starts glowing orange, then melts away, revealing another lava tube behind it.

"Forgive the shoddy entrance you came through yesterday, my friends, but I enjoy my privacy and only keep that entrance open for emergencies, mainly because Hi'iaka insists on it. This is the actual front door."

It's good to know that someone as regal as Pele doesn't have to crawl into her own home. We watch as the passage completely forms, then cools. She rubs her hand along one side of the lava tube, making it glow with a volcanic light. That will certainly help us navigate, even though it's probably just a one-way trip. The goddess begins her walk through the tube, at a brisk pace, which we have a hard time keeping up with.

As we make our way through the tunnel, the temperature rises … probably due to the light, which is probably literally volcano bile. Me and William are both sweating like crazy, but somehow Gabe is looking like normal. Beyond normal: he's drinking another cup of coffee! How can he think of having a hot beverage in the belly of a volcano?

Thankfully, this particular tube is much shorter than the one we traversed to get to Pele's home. Fresh air … this time actual fresh air, not just an air pocket in a mountain … starts to blow on our faces, marking the exit. The wind whips across the mouth of the tube, colder than I would expect in Hawaii, but still welcome. The sweat on our faces is starting to cool and dry off. I can see steam nearby, clearly from another volcanic vent. We're certainly near the surface, that's for sure.

Pele stands out in the midst of the steam, awaiting our emergence from the lava tube. She opens her arms widely toward us. "Welcome to my front porch, my friends. Please watch your steps. Gabe, William, this is as far as you can go."

The three of us extract ourselves from the lava tube and come over to where Pele stands, only stopping when we realize she's on the very edge of a sheer drop. Before us lies a nearly round volcanic crater, smoking and emitting large amounts of heat and sulfuric smells. It's kind of hard to breathe here.

Gabe nods. "Of course. I should have known the gate would be here." He turns toward me and William. "We're at the Kilauea caldera, the crater of the world's most active volcano. This volcano has been erupting continuously for nearly fifty years."

As he says that, we can see a high pillar of lava launch from the center. It splatters all around, orange glowing blotches against the black landscape in the crater. I see the steam rising where the column had shot up.

My blood pressure just dropped. *What in the hell am I thinking?*

Dad's face leaps into the front of my mind, which is suddenly talking to me in Michi's voice. *You're saving your Dad, that's what. Now get your big-girl panties on and do this, goddammit!*

I clutch to William's hand. "I can do this."

He nods and pulls me tight into his arms. "I know you can. I believe in you."

I hug him tightly. I don't want to lose this ... I don't want this to change anything; I still want to love this man when this is over. "Take care of the others."

He whispers in my ear. "I will." He picks me up and kisses me, deeply and desperately, for a long time. When we finally release our lip lock, we're both in tears. His voice is barely a whisper. "I love you, Alanna."

I stroke his cheek. "I love you." It's the first time we've both said it out loud at the same time. Something about that makes me feel very hopeful, despite the circumstances.

Pele places a hand gently on my shoulder. "It's time to go, child."

I nod and drop out of William's embrace, turning toward Gabe. "Swear to me you'll keep them all safe, Gabe. Promise me this, no matter how long I'm down there."

Gabe raises his hand. "On my Employer's Honor, Alanna, you have my word."

I smile shallowly. This is the most I've ever been able to get from Gabe, and it satisfies me. I unfurl my wings and turn toward Pele, cinching two belts tighter around my waist. "Okay, I'm ready to go."

Pele nods. "Stay with me as best as you can." She extends a hand out toward the center of the crater. More lava bubbles up through the rock floor, forming large, orange geysers into the sky. In the center of the activity, I can see an indentation forming, almost like another tube, only this time it's vertical.

Straight down into a fiery abyss.

Pele turns her gaze toward me meaningfully, nods, and then leaps out into the center of the lava. I'm hesitant, but I know she won't wait for me, so I flap my wings and take to the air. It's going to be difficult to get down into the pit because of the hot air wanting to push me further up, but I have to try my best.

My breathing is coming fast. The only words in my mind are from the prayer card Grandmother gave me last year.

Lord in Heaven, Creator of Earth
Remind me what in life has worth ...

I rise against my will. I try to fight the laws of physics, to go down against the hot air, but it's not happening. My heart rate is going up.

Family, friends, all those I love
My shelter 'til I meet You above ...

My muscles strain. I need to follow Pele, I can see her diving deeper into the pit and she's speeding up. I have to get down there. There's only one way it's happening.

And keep me safe 'til the day when
I see them again, in Your name, Amen.

I curl my wings around my body. Without their fleshy parachutes, gravity takes over. I drop quickly, right down into the center of the fire. My last glimpse of any life above the volcano's surface is Gabe, looking as serious as always, and William, whose worry colors his eyes even from this distance.

God help me. I'm going to Hell.

·

Footsteps of Dante

Chapter Eleven: Guides

Day 1

The descent through the lava tube is a long one. Pele is hard to keep in sight as I try to concentrate on keeping myself and my supplies out of the liquid flame that surrounds me, threatens to consume me. It's only through Pele's good graces that it holds at bay, almost like it respects her, although it's weird to think of something mindless like magma obeying a master of any kind.

"Stay with me, child. This is no place to straggle."

My wings have been virtually rendered useless. If I unfurl them, I slow down, and I can't keep up with Pele. On top of that, the passage keeps getting narrower and narrower; I'm convinced that if I even try opening them up, the tips will be singed and then they'll be really useless. My only hope now is that Pele knows what she's doing.

How did I talk myself into this in the first place?

This lava stretches downward, into the earth, for miles and miles. It glows, white-hot in places, pulsing and flowing and bubbling around us, hungering for the taste of flesh. I curl my wings tighter around my body, protectively, wanting to shield myself from the heat.

The ever-present heat is starting to get to me. I'm getting light-headed, and this tunnel continues straight downward, never relenting, never curving. My vision is starting to swim. Pele is getting harder and harder to keep in sight, her flowing robes fluttering around her, almost daring the lava to touch her, even though Pele is its master.

Within the protective cocoon of my wings, I grip the hilt of the Sword tighter. No Guardsman has ever ventured where I'm going. None has even thought to. Yet here I am, half-cocked, following this pathway down into the bowels of existence, hoping that when the time comes and I have to draw the weapon that the power will come to me.

Bringing God to a godless place.

My vision clears suddenly. I now realize that the air temperature is getting slightly cooler, and the lava tunnel is not quite as narrow anymore. I tighten my wings around me and drop faster, getting back up behind Pele where I need to be before slightly opening them up once more to slow my descent. I need to have some modicum of control, especially here.

This time, no control leads to destruction.

With my vision returning to normal, I can now see that the rocky ground is coming up awfully fast. A quick glance around me confirms that the lava is far enough away that I can turn my body, which I do, bringing my feet back down so that they will hit first. Pele is already there, and barely steps aside before I touch down extremely hard, enough to rattle pebbles on the surface. The jarring my knees take on impact, though, is far more worrisome.

"On your feet." Pele's voice becomes commanding and sharp. "We're here."

I nod toward the goddess, shaking out my wings. I should try to retract them ....

I can't. "What's this now?"

Pele seems to understand my confusion, I think. "When you arrive here, whatever form you take is the form you keep for as long as you reside."

That might make things uncomfortable after a while. I try several ways of carrying my wings close to my body before settling on a cape effect around my shoulders. Pele takes no notice of my awkwardness and starts walking away from me, toward one of the lava walls. A brief sweep of her hand parts the molten rock curtain, exposing an opening into impenetrable darkness.

As I watch the part in the lava open further, I notice it's forming something resembling a gate. It appears to be wrought iron and hideous, spiked and decorated with hellish figures, twisted and molded into a grotesque sculpture.

Words form across the top of the doors, formed from gnarled branches.

ABANDON HOPE, YE WHO ENTER HERE

The air around me, which I know to be sizzling hot, chills. A shiver runs down my entire body, like my blood has abandoned me along with hope. "This is it?"

Pele nods solemnly. "I cannot go further, child. It's up to you now. However, Gabe has arranged for an escort inside the gate, who will take you where you need to go."

Escort, huh? Who would possibly want to take this journey along with me? With those questions in my mind, I approach the opening, only stopped by Pele placing her hand reassuringly on my shoulder.

"Those above who still honor me call me goddess of fury, but know this … among the emotions which rule humans, the most intense and powerful are hatred and love. It is impossible for anger to exist without compassion." She squeezes my shoulder. "I wish you luck on you quest, Alanna. Find your father."

I place my hand on the goddess's, returning her show of respect. "I will. Be ready for my return."

Pele nods and turns away, walking into the lava flow and allowing herself to be consumed.

Returning home. Like I will be soon, hopefully.

I take a deep breath, try to slow the pounding of my heart, and step through the gate. The first thing that greets me is the stench. Horrifying smells permeate the air of the place, making it difficult to breathe. Smells like burning ammonia, like excrement and sweat. The unmistakable odor of blood finds my nostrils: far too much has been shed here. My breathing becomes quick pants before I abandon dignity and start mouth-breathing, but even then I can't get away from the horrid smells.

My eyes take longer to adjust than my lungs. When they do, when the darkness is allowed to subside and I can focus, the sight is equally as horrifying as the smell. Emaciated bodies, skin stretched beyond all reason, writhe about on the ground, clawing at the dirt, pleading for release. Their hair has been ripped out of their scalps, occasionally taking chunks of skin. Teeth fall out. The moans of these hideously tortured beings are almost too much for my ears to handle, and their multitude makes my mind want to shut down.

A bony, shredded hand grips my ankle. Eyes that have long since gone sightless look up at me as this pitiful creature tries to climb up my leg. His voice quavers when he speaks.

"You … you live … you bring life here …"

Another slithers up behind the first, climbing over him rudely. "We pray and pray for release, we plead for our souls, but God never answers … please be our salvation …"

The moans of these two are starting to attract attention from the others. More and more of the shambling living corpses crawl over, climb over each other. They're on all sides of me now. I can't get away.

One of them reaches for one of the bottles. I can't let him have it, and I make sure he knows this by punching him in the face. He only backs off for a moment before resuming his quest.

They're after the water. The **holy** *water. The only sign that God exists in this place.*

They threaten to overwhelm me. They're up to my chest. One grasps my shoulder tightly … not the friendly grasp like Pele had given me, but a more forceful one, like he's trying to pull me down with the rest of the group.

"She is not one of yours! Away with you all!"

A commanding voice, which still sounds hollow, echoes from behind me. Clearly, though, these creatures respect its owner, because they all slide back down and into the shadows. I can't see who my benefactor is yet, though, because I'm still focused on getting the monsters off of me. I spread my wings to knock the last of them off.

Time to find out who it is. Maybe he's supposed to be my guide. "Whoever you are, thank you."

I see an upright figure approaching me through the gloom. The voice, much more hollow than it was, continues to speak. "Now that I have seen it, I know that he did not lie to me."

"Gabe, you mean?"

He nods, still in the shadows, but still approaching. Do the shadows ever abate here? "After witnessing what you have done, I know for sure that you are your mother's daughter, that you are the one he mentioned."

"You know my mother?"

He chuckles, in a way that makes me pity him. "'Knew' is probably more correct of a term for it, Alanna Sharpe. I knew Ariel when she was a girl, not much younger than you are now. I knew her mother, I knew your family, and I tried to destroy them. That's why I'm here now."

He comes close to me, and now I can make out his features. This is clearly another soul, another human being paying penance for crimes he committed in life. He's missing one arm, which appears to have just dissolved off of him, a process which seems to be continuing as his upper arm bone protrudes from the stump. He's dressed in what appears to be the remains of a designer suit, and a Rolex watch hangs loosely from the one wrist he has remaining. Another unusual thing about his clothing: draped over his shoulders are twin sashes, which look like priestly vestments.

Then I see his face. Or what's left of it. The right half of it appears to have simply been ripped off of his skull, and the remaining skin is jagged and torn where the wounding took place. Whatever took the skin off left the eyeball, however, and it stares unblinking at me, bloodshot and clearly in need of hydration. What part of his face is left is that of an older man, maybe in his fifties, with mousy brown hair turning gray. His other eye ... the one with an eyelid still ... displays regret, sadness, and guilt, that much I'm certain.

I need to know who this is. "What's your name?"

He sighs. "Only fair you should know. I am your guide in this forsaken land. My name is Alastair Abaster."

The name instantly chills me. I know this name. Alastair Abaster, pastor of the Church of Christian Purity, the man who tried to bring Armageddon early. The man who tried to kill my parents.

The Invader.

"Why would you, of all souls, help me?"

Abaster's face darkens. "I am forever condemned to this ungodly place, Alanna. I blasphemed against God, I used my position of power and influence to commit great sins. Worst of all, I brought Hell upon the earth. I can receive no greater punishment than to be tormented here, away from the light of holiness. I can't possibly live in more torment than I am right now, so it neither profits me nor punishes me to guide you."

That didn't answer my question. "Still, why?"

He sighs. "It is an opportunity to atone for a great wrong, though I know that no amount of atonement will ever relieve the burden of my punishment. What I do know is where your father's soul is, how to get to him, and why he is here." He approaches me quickly. "There is much territory to cross, though, and little time to do it. Your allies in the living world need you to succeed promptly."

He's right about that. I clutch the Sword's hilt. "Where am I right now?"

Abaster motions around the landscape. "This is the vestibule of Hell. Dante referred to it as the first circle, or Limbo."

I flip open the copy of the *Inferno* that Gabe loaned me as a road map, finding the stanzas about Limbo. Something doesn't seem right ... "Dante describes it as a riverbank with a fortress. What is all this?"

Abaster smirks bitterly. "The reality. Dante was way off when he described this place … he only presented what he *thought* the circles of Hell were like, colored by his own perceptions and his era. There may have been a fortress here in his time, but now it's simply a muddy wasteland. He also put the landmarks in the wrong order, for he placed this within Hell proper rather than on the outskirts of it."

I scan the ground around me, looking for more shambling ghouls. Thankfully, Abaster's voice seems to have scared them all away. "What did you do to them just now?"

"Of the things I was allowed to keep from my life, one was my voice. I always took pride in it."

One of the seven deadly sins … why am I not surprised?

Abaster motions into the distance. "The Acheron River, the one Dante mentions, merged with the ground eons ago, creating nothing but this bog. However, you can still cross it in a boat, and we need to give the boatman his due. Come, follow me."

He begins trudging through the thick muck. Keeping one hand on the Sword, I follow him, slowly. The mud doesn't want to give up our feet as we make our way through it. Matter of fact, it seems like it wants to pull us down into it …

A hand rises up out of the earth and latches on my knee. I kick it aside. More of the ghouls are here, and I realize that when I hit a hard place, I'm on someone's head. I also feel my energy level starting to diminish. I'm going to need to rest and recover soon, if we haven't found the boat.

My hand reaches for one of the gallon bottles. Then I hear Gabe's voice in my head. *"This is all of it you can have with you down there. Consume it sparingly."*

I resist the urge to take a drink and focus on following Abaster, though the stories my mother tells run through my mind. Alastair Abaster apparently came into contact with the Sabre and started using it to raise the dead, forming them into an army which attacked via bodies of water. A showdown took place at the Church of Christian Purity, which led to the appearance of Abaddon, the biggest demon Mom and Dad ever fought. Abaddon was defeated, but not before Dad was seriously hurt.

Suddenly I want to know more about the battle. Though it should probably wait until we get a calm moment. *If* we get a calm moment.

Abaster stirs me from my memory. "He's just up ahead. Come on!"

We speed up as best as we can through the knee-high loam, until at last we're at the remains of a pier. I can clearly see that the mud beyond the pier is far more liquid, as it bubbles and shifts constantly. Like he said, there's a boat … a skiff, really … sitting at the pier, with a shrouded figure holding a steering pole standing atop it. The figure raises a hand … a bony, skeletal hand … and motions for us to stop.

"Boatman, take us across to Minos. We have business within."

The boatman's voice is a hoarse creak. "You, perhaps. Her, no. She lives still."

Abaster groans. "Alanna Sharpe is on a holy quest, boatman. You cannot refuse her passage."

"I can, and I will, vessel of Abaddon. You are in no position to bargain."

I approach the boatman, tightening my grip on the Sword. "I was sent here by Gabe Francis. I'm here to reclaim my father's soul."

The face of the man, hidden under his hood, still darkens. "I don't care. No mortal shall cross on my skiff."

I don't know whether I should threaten him or not. After all, he's only doing his job. I step on the boat, despite his protestations.

"Take us across. Our business is on the other side." Abaster's voice is level, but still has power.

"The hell I will!" The boatman whips off his hood, and now I can see that he's an elderly man, missing his teeth and hair, with eyes sunken into his skull. Clearly he has spent far too long doing this. "I have my responsibilities! After I brought that Dante fellow across, Minos had my liver for lunch, he was that angry. I don't give a damn whether it was God Himself who sent her ..."

"It was." I draw the Sword as proof.

I'm used to the Guardswoman enclosing around me, putting me into a protective embrace, wrapping me in armor. Instead, the only thing that happens is that my arms bulk up and I find myself wielding the Sword while wearing two forearm-length metal gauntlets. The point of the Sword is what I'm more interested in, though, and it's dangling threateningly close to the boatman's Adam's apple.

Can I speak here with the Sword drawn? Usually the Guardswoman is mute. Might as well try.

"Now are you going to take us across or not?"

My voice surprises everyone present, not the least myself. It's the dragon's growl, magnified to the nth degree. The boatman is suddenly on his knees, hands up by his shoulders.

"Please don't hurt me ... I'll take you ... I didn't know I was dealing with a Guardsman ..." He's nearly weeping with fear.

I sheathe the Sword, and the entire world spins. The gauntlets disappear from my arms, but I feel like I just got kicked in the head by a horse. I still have the presence of mind, however, to talk to the boatman. "It's okay. I know it's just your job." I put a hand on his shoulder ... partly to reassure him and partly to keep my balance.

He sniffles, smiles weakly, then stands up and motions to Abaster to come aboard. Once everyone is on the skiff, the boatman dips his pole into the liquid muck and starts ferrying us across.

My head is still swimming ... and my breathing is speeding up. Instinctively, I reach for one of the bottles of holy water, open it, and take a small sip. Though the liquid's presence in my system is taking away my dizziness, I still feel very fatigued. Maybe the strain of the trip is starting to get to me. Whatever the case, it's all I can do to lie down on the floor of the skiff, wrapped in my wings, and sleep.

Chapter Twelve: Minos

Day 2

When I rouse from my unconscious, exhausted sleep, the boat is just pulling up on the opposite "shore" of the Limbo bog. My head feels much clearer, and I sit up and make my way next to Abaster.

"How long have I been sleeping?"

"About a day. There isn't much you have missed, Alanna, just the voyage across Limbo."

The boatman makes one last, strong push with his skiff pole, driving the boat up on the more firm ground. "Here we are, as requested. The Court of Minos."

I should show some appreciation … after all, he risked his neck for me. I gently embrace the boatman. "Thank you for taking us across."

I don't think he's used to any sort of affection, but he tries to return the hug in kind. "I wish you luck and Godspeed in your quest, Guardsman."

Abaster is waiting for me by the door of a massive building, carved into a cave. The passageway has to be a hundred feet tall and at least that wide. I'm staggered by the sheer magnitude of this door, and almost don't notice when it opens for Abaster, who waves to me to follow him. The interior of the building is just as gigantic in scale as the door, reaching up what seems like an infinite height. The darkness above my head completely obscures the ceiling of this place … if it even has a ceiling.

Once I've adjusted to the scale of the room, I finally focus on the room's sole occupant, at the opposite end. Abaster makes a motion toward him.

"Minos."

The creature at the opposite end of the hallway is just as titanic as the room itself. By my estimate, he has to stand at least three hundred feet tall, and seems to only loom larger the closer we approach. He has a bull's head, topping a heavily muscled body, with a long tail whipping back and forth behind him. As we approach, his eyes narrow toward us.

"Alastair Abaster, you have already faced judgment. Why do you approach again?"

Abaster seems a bit shaken, but he stands his ground. "Minos, I act on God's behalf as a guide for this mortal."

Minos's eyes narrow further. "I know this mortal. Alanna Sharpe, the Guardsman, you do not belong here. Be warned, should you continue, you shall face the full horrors of Hell, just as the damned do."

I guess I need to state my case. I step forward. My hand hasn't left the Sword's hilt yet. "Your Honor, I don't take this journey lightly. There is a soul currently trapped in Hell, the soul of a Guardsman, who should not be here, and I have been tasked with his rescue."

Minos seems unmoved. "One's status as a Guardsman guarantees you nothing. Do you not think that I have seen Sharpes come through? The birthright does not automatically create a righteous soul."

"Make no mistake, Minos, I do not have any illusions that there are no Sharpes in Hell. I'm sure some in my family line abused their power as the Guardsman. This particular soul did not, though. He does not deserve damnation, he has not earned it."

The judge rumbles and stands up. *Oh my God, he was sitting down! He's humongous and he's approaching!!*

Abaster steps in front of me, protectively. As he approaches, I can see that Minos isn't looking too welcoming. His eyes are turning red. The hooves that comprise his feet are shaking the ground with every step.

"Who are you to preclude my judgment? I am the sole judge of Hell. Mine has been a role I have kept for centuries, never once has a soul gone through this room without my attention!"

His voice is a bull's bellow. His breath tries to knock me backward. Despite the struggle, I hold my ground, clutching the Sword's hilt tighter. I grit my teeth and respond. "As much as I respect you, Minos, you are wrong in this instance. Cole Sharpe is not a soul deserving of this. He was my father. He was a good man, a righteous man who used the power of the Guardsman to defend life, not to magnify himself."

Minos's face takes on a puzzled expression. "Cole Sharpe? He did not pass through here."

"Yet his soul resides in Hell currently. How did he get in there without you having judged his soul?"

Abaster approaches at my left side. "Hear me, Lord Minos. Alanna Sharpe comes on an errand for He Who Is Called I AM. She must be allowed to continue into the abyss."

Minos's shoulders slump slightly. He shakes his head, like he's trying to clear his own confusion physically. He snuffs, and a warm blast of air comes out of his nose. Finally, he stamps one of his hooved feet.

"Very well. Alanna Sharpe, you will be allowed passage without judgment. Be warned, though, as I said before, you will face the full punishments of the damned. Hell can make no exceptions for the righteous."

I kneel gently. I'm not sure if that's the right thing to do, but it seems respectful. "Thank you."

"Also be advised, Alastair Abaster notwithstanding, you will not pass through this court again. To leave Hell, it is a one-way journey. The deeper you go in, the fiercer the dangers. Gird your soul for the torments which beckon."

My free hand wanders to one of the bottles. "Lord Minos, I can assure you ... nothing in Hell compares to the torments which I have already lived through. Thank you for the warning, though." I motion toward Abaster. "Lead on."

Abaster bows toward Minos as well before guiding me through the darkness and further into the abyss. The opposite door of Minos's court finally appears through the dusky gloom, and opens for us. Once we pass through, however, I hear the oppressive slam of the door and turn around, but no door is cut into the wall anymore. My hands feel along the stone wall, allowing the dark mist to conceal me.

Abaster's hand on my shoulder stops my search. "Minos did warn you, we will not pass through his court again. Come, we must continue."

I give up my search for the door and come up to Abaster's side. "Where are we now?"

He clears his throat. "The ring immediately adjacent to the Court of Minos holds those most guilty of the sin of Lust." He crouches down on the ground. "You might want to take cover."

I realize why a little too late, as a giant gust of wind catches within my wings and flings me quickly away from Abaster. He reaches to grab me, but reaches with the wrong arm ... the one missing a hand ... and can't catch me. The wind is too inconsistent, and buffers me about like a plastic bag in a tornado.

Through my confusion, I can hear voices around me, shrieks and cries for mercy. I try to open my eyes, and catch a glimpse of several naked men and women, similarly blown about like I am, only they occasionally smash against the wall of the Court of Minos. I hear from that direction screams of a different sort ... screams of rage, screams of anger, all of it directed toward Minos for sentencing them to this circle.

My stomach is rotating in the opposite direction as I'm being blown ... I have to take control of this situation! I grit my teeth, close my eyes, and force my wings to use the wind rather than act as a parachute in it. After fighting for precious seconds and clutching my stomach to prevent myself from getting sick, I finally can feel myself getting back to an upright position, under somewhat control. I dare to open my eyes and find myself far up above the surface, so high that I feel like I'm completely obscured in a cloud of shadow.

By gauging the wind's direction based on the souls I see flying past, I'm finally able to get some navigational control. I tilt my wings, searching for currents, while scanning the ground in search of Abaster. When I finally spot him, he's standing and waving toward me. I cape my wings around myself and enter a fast descent, tilting myself away from the harsh wind gusts, until I'm close enough to safely touch down. I remain in a crouched position, though, and approach Abaster.

"You sound like someone who's been here before. How did you know ...?"

"I'm no stranger to these winds." Abaster shows me his remaining hand, which appears to be raw. "The sands of Hell blow through those winds, and rend flesh on those souls who are being punished in Circle 2. I've had my fair share of sandblasting in my time here."

I stroke my chin slightly. "So exactly *where* in Hell did you come from?"

Abaster sighs. "It's complicated. I may tell you about it sometime. In the meantime, let us continue ... you have a father to find."

I nod and try to brush myself off, though I doubt I'll be successful. "All right. So all of these souls here are those of the primarily lustful?"

Abaster nods as we walk through the circle. More souls soar overhead, screaming as they pass over us. "These are the souls of those with no self-control where it comes to matters of sex. They are the lustful, those who gave in to their animal side rather than that of reason."

Spoken like one who knows ... but I won't say anything. Yet. "How many souls wind up here?"

He shrugs. "Hard to say, no one's ever tried taking a census." He looks around, then crouches again and pulls me down with him. "Look over there, girl. Do you see those men over there?"

I look across the plain from where we are crouched and see seven men, all stripped naked, all of them whipped and bruised and beaten. They are all red, whipped raw by the sand flying in the air. They are also all bound, chained down to anchors on the ground. Then I notice the line of demons behind them, all of them in various states of arousal ...

"Good God ... what the hell is going on over there?"

Abaster smirks. "An apt way of putting it, Alanna. Those seven men were commanders in the Jerzaanian Royal Guard, who served their master by capturing, enslaving, and raping women. They gave in to the sin of lust, using the excuse of duty. Their punishment here is to be eternally raped by a never-ending parade of demons."

I hear each of the men scream as the next demon starts in on them. The demons only cruelly chuckle. One growls and takes a bite out of a man's shoulder while having its way with him.

"And the chains?"

"A fitting punishment as well. If they were normal lustful souls, they would be blown around by the winds of Circle 2. Those chains ensure that they never have respite from this punishment that they rightly deserve. When the winds come, they are picked up by it, but the chains around their neck strangle them and keep them held down to that place."

Another man screams, like no other male scream I've ever heard. I can feel the warmth in my eyes ...

"Do not cry for them, Alanna."

I sigh and try to collect myself. "I hate watching people suffer, you have to understand that."

"I do, and that's what makes you a good Guardsman, and a good person. But you must understand ... these men suffer because they have earned this, this is the wage of their great sin."

Too much suffering ... I've seen too many people suffer at the hands of the New Empire. Too many of my friends and loved ones, being tortured, being threatened ... even as I watch, even as I remember the stories I've been told about Jerzaan, about what their Sovereign did to Aunt Kitty, I still can't help but feel sorry for these men.

Another man's scream is cut off by having something shoved into his mouth, and that's when I reach my emotional limit. I curl up in a shaking ball, trying to hide my face from the horror around me. Abaster seems understanding, as he places an arm around my shoulders. At some point, though I'm too numb to understand it, he helps me to my feet and guides me away.

Chapter Thirteen: Cerberus

Day 3

At some point in Circle 2, I must have passed out, because the next thing I know Abaster is awakening me. I'm still a little groggy … maybe I need another sip … but I'm quickly on my feet. The wind isn't howling, either with its intensity or souls being carried in it, wherever it is we are now.

"Why did you let me sleep?"

Abaster sighs. "You needed the rest, Alanna. Be on guard now, we're crossing into the next circle and must pass by its guardian."

I tighten my grip on the Sword, but keep it at my hip as we walk forward, deeper into the darkness. Abaster remains in front of me, either guiding me or defending me from whatever we are approaching. I decide that I'll allow him to take the lead for the time being, since he knows far more about Hell than I ever hope to.

A low-pitched rumble catches my attention. I feel threatened … my wings quickly come out, surrounding both me and Abaster. I'm ready for action now.

"We need to be careful, Alanna. We're approaching Circle 3's guardian, and convincing him we can pass will be no easy task."

I can't help thinking that the rumble sounds kind of familiar. "What kind of guardian is it? Human, animal … demonic?"

"Last two. Just trust me." Abaster continues to step with measured paces. I take a moment as we're walking to pull out the *Inferno,* to find out what's approaching.

The name stops me short. *Cerberus.*

That explains the rumble … it's growling … and it's getting louder as we continue forth.

My breathing accelerates, but Abaster's pace never slackens. He continues moving forward at a quick clip, and I'm hard-pressed to keep up with him. Ultimately, we emerge from the perpetual dusty shadow of Circle 2 and into a wide plain of muddy bogs, pounded upon by a frigid rain.

"Great, more mud," I mutter.

I shouldn't have said anything. The words are no sooner out of my mouth before a giant three-headed mastiff bounds across the plain, all three heads baying and barking at us. Clearly this creature is not happy to see us. One head growls, another barks, and the third, central head reaches out to us and tries to bite.

On instinct, I pull the Sword out of its sheath. The gauntlets wrap around my arms once more, and I hold the weapon out so that Cerberus can see it.

I'm getting weak too quickly ... I have to do it now ...

I take a swing with the Sword and catch the middle head across the snout. It yelps and backs away from me, while the other two lunge. I flap my wings once and jump over their attack, leaving them gnawing at each other's teeth. My attempt at a smooth landing behind the dog doesn't go too well, though, and I stumble as the mud catches my feet and doesn't let me slide. I fight the imbalance but finally get upright.

"Now let us pass, doggie!"

Cerberus doesn't notice me, because he's too busy licking his wound. The dog whimpers, scratching at the cut I put across his middle nose, and runs off.

My heart is pounding too quickly. I sheathe the Sword and reach for the already-opened gallon of holy water, taking three swallows and trying to stand still until I feel more like myself. While I pant and catch my breath, Abaster comes up behind me.

"You didn't have to do that, you know. Cerberus only needed distraction, not injury."

"I panicked. Can you blame me?" The words come out sounding angrier than I intend, partly because of my shortness of breath. "So where are we now?"

"We're deep within Circle 3 now, Alanna. In this circle resides the gluttonous."

My breathing is slowing down enough that I can start using my senses to be aware of my surroundings again. One of the first sensations that reaches me is the smell … the smell of festering flesh, of rotting garbage, of mold and vomit, like a concentration of millions of port-a-johns. My stomach's threatening me again, but I fight it.

"Is that why this place smells like a cesspool?"

Abaster nods. "It is. The sinners here could not control their baser impulses when it came to food and drink and alcohol, and as a result they are here. You can see them if you look around."

I take his advice and scan the ground around us. There are a lot of lumps in the ground, fleshy lumps that look like bloated corpses. The whole landscape is disgusting, and then I hear the first fart.

And we have to cross through this morass …

I feel the bile rising in my throat as I allow Abaster to lead me forward. I doubt I'll need the Sword here, but it's a comfort to keep my hand on it, almost like a security blanket. The rain continues to fall on us, with some of it turning hard like hail. I keep my wings wrapped around myself, trying to conserve my body heat. It's hard to do as the mud begins to penetrate through my shoes, giving me chills.

How much is mud and how much is …

My stomach gurgles. Abaster must have heard it, because he's turning around toward me. "Don't worry, Alanna, we won't be in this Circle too much longer. Try to hold it in, otherwise we will attract unwanted attention."

I think we've already done that, though, because one of the bloated souls lying in the mud around us opens his eyes and kind of slithers … on his back … toward us. The soul's distended belly makes it look like a whale swimming through the mud. The eyes are hollow and decomposed as they look up at me. Then the soul opens his mouth, and the extent of the decay to his body is evident as his mouth only contains four teeth and a green tongue.

"Living soul … feed us, we hunger for life …"

His bloated hand, like an oversized baby's hand, reaches out of the mud and tries to grab my knee. I dodge the slow swipe and kick the hand away. "You don't look like you need any more …"

"We must feed … we hunger …" Another soul joins the first, floating in the mud. Abaster has noticed my predicament and is coming back for me, but he's having trouble fighting through the souls.

One puts a hand on my shoulder and pulls. I feel myself being yanked into the thick muck, its chill penetrating my entire body. Another soul climbs on top of me, her dead, empty eyes showing greed and hunger as she tries to bite me.

I punch the soul climbing over the top of me to knock her off. I kick hard toward the other souls, trying to keep them away from me. I almost feel like it's a lost cause until I feel one of the souls being dragged off of me. Sitting up in the muck I look over toward where that soul was pulled and see Cerberus, the sinner in the jaws of his left head, shaking the soul like a dog toy. The other souls realize that Cerberus is standing there and flee … apparently the dog must do this a lot … and are rewarded by having the three-headed mastiff chase them around.

Abaster grabs my arm and helps me free myself from the muck … which coats me from head-to-toe. I try to push as much of the crap off of me as I can, but it's saturated my clothes, my shoes … I doubt the smell's going away anytime soon. Three days in, and I need a bath.

How much of the water can I use, though? I don't want to douse myself in it, but I need to do something.

Experimentally, I open one of the bottles, pour a small amount on my fingertips, and use it to make the sign of the Cross on my forehead.

It's like being doused by a holy fire hose. The muck flies off of my body, finally allowing me to feel clean for the first time in hours. I flap my wings slightly, lifting off a couple of feet to free my feet from the muck, and watch as they, too, shake off the thick mud.

Flying is taking its toll on me, though ... there's not a lot of wind current in this Circle, so I have to flap nearly constantly to remain in the air. I dip down and lift Abaster up from the sty by his elbows.

"What are you doing?"

I call down to him, "Speeding things up. We're heading for Circle 4, right? Lead the way."

Abaster sighs and points. "That way. Follow the road."

When I look past the hanging soul's body, I see that there's a road ... badly marked and barely there ... which winds through Circle 3, until it reaches another gate. Beyond the gate, I can't see anything, which is worrisome.

I bring myself into a slow descent, although to do it I can't just glide like normal. My wings are thoroughly exhausted when I finally alight and land, just on the inside of the gate. Thankfully, the ground is more solid than in the sty, so I set down Abaster and collapse, panting.

Abaster helps me to an upright sitting position. "We'll rest here. You'll need your strength for the next circle."

I lean against the wall just next to the gate's hinge. My breathing just won't calm down. I don't want to use any more water today ... I pluck the one bottle from my belt and see that there's about a third of it already gone. Trying to distract myself as I return the bottle to my belt, I look over to Abaster. "So you seem to know a lot about every circle of this place."

He nods, kind of sadly, and sits down close by. "I too have read the *Inferno,* Alanna."

I narrow my eyes. "I think it's more than that."

His eyes ... at least the one behind a fleshy face ... look surprised, then finally repentant. "You're too good at detecting dishonesty."

"I've had a lot of practice lately," I spit back bitterly. "So talk. We've got nothing better to do tonight."

Abaster sighs, clutching his half-gone arm with his one remaining hand. "I told you it was complicated, Alanna. My sins in life were complex, more than just Four Corners."

"Seems like Four Corners was the worst of it, though ..."

"True, but it was ... I don't know how to say it, but it was the capper of a lot of other crimes I had committed against God." He shifts around, like he's uncomfortable. "In life, I was a pastor, a minister. I brought the Word of God to those in need of comfort and counsel, mainly around the Navajo reservation. This is how I met your grandmother, and your mother.

"As my congregation grew, more and more people came from far away to see me. Eventually I was approached by a television producer, who wanted to put my services on the air. In my arrogance and naiveté, I accepted. More people heard my message, more people came to Christ through my ministry.

"I realize now that I couldn't handle the influx of followers. I thought I was a Messiah, but all I turned out to be was an Antichrist."

I scratch my head. "You mentioned several crimes ..."

He nods. "I adultered and overspent ... I used my church's monies to enhance my own image, to create the image of the wealthy ... I purchased women for sexual purposes."

My opinion of my guide is really starting to drop ... even lower than it already was. "So you were basically a money-grubbing old sex addict."

Abaster chuckles. "Oh, if it were only that. I committed my greatest crime when I found a mysterious weapon, touring an archaeology dig in Syria. After doing some research, I found out about the Guardsman and about the Sword …"

This calls for a facepalm. "So naturally, since you thought you were God's gift to the world, you assumed that *you* were the Guardsman."

"I did, and that was one of my greatest crimes against the Almighty. My punishment for that blasphemy, however, does not compare to that for my ultimate crime." His voice lowers. "When I brought the undead to the world of the living … when I tried to enact Abaddon's plans … the punishments for these sins trifles against the punishment I serve for killing a Guardsman."

My heart races. My throat clamps up. "What do you …?"

Abaster sighs. "During the final battle in Four Corners, I murdered your father."

Chapter Fourteen: Ursus Sharpe

Day 4

I could not stand to talk any longer with Abaster after his confession. I was mad at him ... still am, really ... and so I went to sleep, to try to recover my energy.

As I awaken now, I'm still angry with him, but I realize I'm also angry with my parents, and with Gabe. Why didn't they tell me the story this way? Why didn't they tell me that Dad actually *died* at Four Corners?

Something doesn't add up. If Dad died at Four Corners, how did he spend all of my life with me? How did I know my father, when, if Abaster is correct, he was killed even before I was born? Swallowing my anger, I decide I'll find out ... Abaster approaches me quickly.

"Come, Alanna, we must cross through Circle 4."

I stand up, a little wobbly, and cross my arms, shooting Abaster my best angry glare. "First thing's first, Abaster. If you killed my father, then how did I grow up with him?"

He shrugs. "I'm not entirely clear on it. I know that Abaddon was defeated by your *mother* taking up the Sword. I know that some sort of miracle took place which brought your father back. The details are fuzzy, since by that time I was already in Minos's courtroom facing judgment."

He seems to know a bit about the situation ... maybe he'll be able to answer my doubts. "Why would Mom lie to me about those events? About Dad being killed, why would she hide something like that? Why would Gabe?"

Abaster smiles and approaches me. "Oh dear, Alanna, as mature as you are I forget that you are still, in some ways, yet a child." Even though I'm wary of it, he places his hand on my shoulder. "Most likely, your mother and your friend only gave you half-truths about the situation because they felt you didn't need to know about it, being a young girl.

I'm sure your mother decided that, since your father was there, all you needed to know was that he was wounded."

I suppose it makes sense. Why tell a little girl her dad died and then got resurrected? I didn't need to know until I was mature enough ... and even then I doubt I'm even mature enough now. I decide to set the matter aside for later, and come up to Abaster's side, looking at the next door.

He motions with his stump arm. "On the other side of this door are those who are guilty of the sin of greed. Although we will not find your father there, we must cross through it to continue on our path."

I open up the *Inferno* again as Abaster pounds on the door. "Plutus! Let us pass!"

The door slowly swings out toward us, and out steps what appears to be a normal-sized man. Then I see that his skin is entirely encased in precious metals and gemstones. I check the book and realize that Plutus is also called Pluto, so befitting the Roman god of wealth he's blinged out his entire body.

Plutus approaches and smiles, and I can see grotesque diamonds that encrust his teeth. "Ahh, Alastair Abaster. Back for more?"

Abaster's face darkens. "I'm here on a holy errand. We must be allowed to pass through."

The glittering Plutus approaches me. I keep a hand tightly on the Sword. The guard chuckles and leers in my direction. "I'll let you through, girlie, for a proper price."

My voice becomes a snarl. "What price would that be?"

He reaches for the Sword. Before I can stop him, his metallic hand clutches the hilt, trying to wrestle it out of my grasp. "Give it here, girl. Pay the piper, and all."

Abaster is pleading with Plutus to let me pass. He doesn't need to. I draw the Sword and swing wildly at the jewel-encrusted man, trying to back him off. I feel the Sword make purchase in his glittering flesh, and he leaps backward, clutching his chest in pain. It's only when I get both hands on the Sword that I look up toward my opponent.

He bleeds, but it's not blood. It's too bubbly.

"She's got some spice to her, Abaster, not like some of your other conquests!"

I growl ... the dragon's growl ... and put the blade of the Sword firmly under Plutus's chin, lifting his face up. This close, I can smell that the substance pouring out of his wound is actually champagne. *"Call me a whore again, bastard. Come on! I DARE YOU!"*

Abaster pushes his way between us, but the Sword never leaves Plutus's neck. "Will you let us pass, gatekeeper? I'm sure you don't want to go through eternity without a head."

Plutus grumbles audibly, but pushes the blade away from him. "Fine then. But you only get one freebie. This way." He motions and leads us through the gate, still clutching his champagne wound. I sheathe the Sword and immediately feel dizzy. Without thinking, I reach for the open bottle of holy water and chug three large swallows.

My head is clearer, but this only makes me worry as I look at the bottle and realize that I've consumed over half of it. *I only have two spares. I need to make this last, if I'm to last this entire trip.*

Plutus guides us through the wall and into the next circle, but the glistening coming through the opening is nearly blinding. Brighter than a thousand suns. I shield my eyes from the glare, but Abaster and Plutus continue as normal.

"Where are we?" I insistently ask my guide.

Abaster turns and sees my discomfort. "Just entering Circle 4, where the hoarders and wasters are punished. Try to keep up."

I jog slightly to bring myself up to the same level as Abaster. Plutus eventually breaks off from the two of us and returns to his post at the circle's entrance. "Why is it so bright here?"

"It's the punishment of all who are sent here. Look around you."

My eyes are starting to adjust to the brightness, so I look around and find myself in the midst of what appears to be a field full of golden statues. But they're not statues, because they're moving, albeit very slowly. They all look like little copies of Plutus.

"What goes on here?" I pull out the book and find our location. "This isn't the punishment Dante mentioned."

"This is one point where Dante diverges from what's here. What you see are the souls of the greedy, the avaricious ... hoarders and wasters, all. Dante's perception was that they all bore heavy weights, which they pushed around, but the truth was worse than he could articulate." Abaster brings me closer to one of the souls. "These souls cannot act against you, because the burden of their sins is too great. These souls were once wealthy men and women, who either hoarded their wealth and gave nothing of themselves, or squandered their money on fripperies. As a result, when they come here, they are doomed to wear their fortunes like another skin."

I stroke my chin. "So Dante wrote it as pushing weights because ... too many people would've thought wearing a solid gold birthday suit would be a good thing?"

Abaster nods. "It was a much different time, Alanna."

The soul Abaster brought us close to narrows his eyes. "I ... know your ... weapon, child."

I spin and have my hand on the Sword, ready for action, but the soul simply stands in front of me, immobilized by what appears to be three tons of molten gold encasing every nook and cranny of his skin. His mouth and face seems to be able to move, though ... I suppose that's so the punishers can have the benefit of watching the tortured suffer.

"If you know the weapon, you probably know what I can do with it, buddy."

There's a barely-perceptible nod. "I know, child. I bore it."

Oh no ... this is a hellbound Sharpe! I narrow my eyes. "Who are you?"

"In life, I was known as Ursus Sharpe. I was a landowner, a lord, with servants and peasants in my holdings. For a while, I was the wealthiest man in the world ..."

Ursus trails off slightly. I turn to Abaster. "Why have I never heard of him? Dad told me a lot about the Sword's history and its holders, but never about this guy."

"The sinners here did nothing noteworthy in their lives, other than having great wealth. They did nothing for others that they could not profit from. As a result, an additional part of their punishment is anonymity in the living world."

I have a sudden need to know more about this ancestor of mine. "Ursus, can you tell me when you lived?"

Ursus sputters back to attentiveness. "During the time of the plague. I was commissioned by my king to lead a new Crusade to the Holy Land ... it never came to be, though, because we could not agree on a price."

I groan. No wonder he's here ... he can't see past his own damn wallet. I notice that his hand is slowly moving, approaching the Sword's hilt again.

"Please, Sharpe child, let me hold my Sword once more ... I earned the birthright, I was a Sharpe ..."

I turn the Sword hip away from Ursus. "You keep your hands off of it. You're here for a reason." My voice goes cold the more I speak to this golden man. "You're unknown for a reason, Ursus. You had your chance, and instead you chose to sell the Guardsman to the highest bidder ... and as a result you did *nothing* to prove yourself worthy of the birthright." I turn quickly to Abaster. "Let's go. I don't want to stay in this ring any longer than I need to ... truthfully, I'd prefer the hogs in the Circle 3 pigsty to this place."

Ursus looks disappointed, but my mind is made up about him. Abaster leads me further down the road, through the rest of this circle. As we continue, Ursus's voice never reduces in volume, as he calls out to us and begs to know my price for the Sword.

The Sword is priceless. The fewer Guardsmen like Ursus there are in the line, the better.

Ursus' yelling is getting the attention of other greedy souls around us. Some of them shamble up, the heavy gold coating them forcing slow motion, and reach for us. I try to knock them aside. Some of them get the hint and move away … others, when I hit them, don't even flinch.

I put my back to Abaster's, keeping pace with him as he continues to force his way through the wealthy damned. I throw a kick at a gold woman trying to grab my ankle.

"The Sword is mine, youngling, and I will take back what is mine!"

Damn. It's Ursus, and now I realize what he's doing. He's getting the other souls to slow us down enough for him to catch up and steal the Sword away from me. The longer they stall us, the more they fight, the harder it is to beat them away from us without drawing the Sword and the closer Ursus gets. Eventually the gold-encrusted souls clutch both me and Abaster tightly, preventing us from continuing.

"Ursus, stop this!" Abaster calls out to him. "He Who Is Called I AM was once your master! Heed my words, your descendant acts on His behalf here and you do yourself no favors by interfering with her."

Ursus laughs. "Please. The Guardsman is simply a weapon, nothing more, and beholden to whoever is his master." He's face-to-face with me, his voice creating a low growl. "You, woman, you are no Guardsman. You're no heir. You're no Sharpe."

I glare bullets through Ursus's face. "I'm *fifty times* the Sharpe you are, monster."

He simply grins. His teeth are silver. "We'll see." He reaches for my right hip, clutching the Sword in his grip. He pulls on it.

It doesn't move.

The sheath has a snap flap that can go over the finger guard to secure the Sword in place, but it's not engaged. Ursus pulls. He grasps it with his other hand, then with both hands. Nothing he does can remove the weapon from my side.

I can't help but laugh. "Who's not a Sharpe now?"

Ursus growls again. "What trickery is this?"

"No tricks," Abaster booms. "The Sword only recognizes one master."

Ursus suddenly recoils, looking like he's been bitten. I catch a glimpse of the palm of his hand, which had been gripping at the Sword. The gold encrusting his palm is melted, in an exact pattern to the Sword's hilt.

Dust is pouring out of the wound.

Ursus panics. He clutches his hand, trying to hold the dust inside. "Help me, you fools! What am I paying you for?"

The other souls who had been restraining us rush over to Ursus, which gives me and Abaster a chance to escape. We run away quickly, heading toward as close to a marked border there is to this ring, a riverbank.

"What was happening?" I ask breathlessly.

Abaster's arms pump hard as we run. "Once a soul comes to Hell, it's no longer human. Especially with him, he tried to reclaim the birthright and could not because he's a demon now."

Doesn't that make you a demon, too? I stop myself from asking this question. "Is that why he started leaking dust?"

We finally reach the riverbank. Abaster pulls up and looks at me strangely. "Yes. When the Sword kills demons, they become less than nothing. They become shiftless dust, without form or purpose, and blow away in the wind." He places a hand on my shoulder. "Congratulations ... you just killed a demon."

I look back toward where we had run from. Ursus is simply standing there. The other souls have abandoned him and moved away. I narrow my eyes, trying to focus the telescopic sight the dragon gives me on the wealthy soul, and finally find him coming into focus. Where once he had a face, there is now an expressionless, faceless slab of gold.

I destroyed him. The Sword has destroyed a demon in Hell.

Chapter Fifteen: Styx

Day 5

Sleep doesn't come for me, especially not after dealing with Ursus, so I urge Abaster to continue leading me. Although he tries to insist on us stopping, he relents and motions in front of him, toward the next Circle. No wall greets us, no guardian, nothing. I'm surprised by this ... every previous Circle has had a guardian, at least.

I'm only aware we're in a new circle when I feel the texture of the ground change beneath my feet. It's squishy again. I'm dreading more of Circle 3's excremental filth, but it smells less repulsive, although it's no less dirty.

Abaster motions for me to keep up with him. "We are in Circle 5 now, Alanna. This circle is reserved for the slothful and wrathful."

I scratch my head gently at this. "Both in one Circle? I would have expected the wrathful to be in their own place."

"Certain ones are, actually. These you see around you, these are the minor wrathful souls. They writhe in the mud, while their slothful counterparts perpetually drown in the muck."

I pull out the *Inferno* again, tossing forward pages. "Did Dante see this?"

Abaster nods. "He did. The slothful also bottle anger, which is why they are in this ring along with the openly raging. We can't stay here for very long, there's another obstacle to cross ahead."

I jog slightly to catch up, although I can feel my energy level dropping. I really don't want to ingest any more of the holy water, especially since, if Dante's correct, the worst is yet to come. I try to keep pace with Abaster, and soon we're at a tower, planted into the mud on an unseen foundation.

Abaster slaps his one hand on the tower's wall. A light appears at the top, shining across the murky body of water we've reached. It cuts through the darkness like a knife, and in its beam I can now see another boat approaching, paddled by another boatman.

Great, more boats.

"Where are we right now?"

Abaster turns to face me. "On the outer bank of the River Styx. Our ride is approaching, we must cross this river."

Styx ... Dad mentioned the Styx in his mutterings ... he must have crossed here.

Or is he here right now?

I scan around quickly, hoping to find some sign of Dad, but seeing nothing. The boat pulls up to the shore, and I take in the boatman, in a similar outfit to the one that took us through Circle 1. His face is curled into an eternal scowl, and I can see that the lines in his face seem to have been literally cut into it, enough to draw blood. I shudder at the thought.

The boatman narrows his eyes, and his voice is a creak. "You are mine, soul. You belong to me. I have much to show you about the ways of pain."

Abaster steps between me and the boatman. "Phlegyas, no. She's not yours. She's on a holy errand from He Who Is Called I AM, you cannot have her." To emphasize the point, I simply flash the Sword's hilt toward the boatman.

He grumbles loudly. "Damned living souls, why must you come ruin my fun? What does a guy have to do to blow off a little steam?" His grumbling escalates into a full-throated scream without words.

"That's your problem," Abaster admonishes, "not ours. Take us across."

Phlegyas glares at us, then sarcastically motions toward the two seats in the boat. "Welcome aboard. I'm your host, Captain Phlegyas I-Don't-Give-A-Shit-About-Your-Quest. I swear, you cross me and I'll dump you overboard faster than you can say 'Apollo can kiss my ass.' Let's go already!"

Charming fellow, really. It's when we enter the boat that I notice a distinct difference between myself and Abaster. When he sits down, the boat barely moves. When *I* sit down, though, the boat reacts to the change in weight and displaces some of the Styx waters. Phlegyas visibly struggles with pushing the boat away from the shore, but eventually we make our way into the further open waters of the river.

As we glide over the surface of the water, I become aware of faces, limbs, and bodies sunken beneath the surface of the river, glaring up at me, reaching up, all of them angry. I try to keep myself away from the edges of the boat: the last thing I need is any of these souls grabbing my water supply, or the Sword.

One soul's head bobs out of the water and looks up at us. "You are different ... you are a living soul!"

Damn.

He floats over toward the boat, keeping pace with Phlegyas's paddling. He reaches a hand up toward me. "Living soul, tell me if I'm remembered!"

I grit my teeth and kick him in the face. Unfortunately, he's ready for that and the arm that was previously gripping the boat now has a firm hold on my leg, dragging me off the boat and into the water. I barely hear Abaster cry out my name before I'm submerged, trapped within the writhing bodies of the wrathful souls doomed to swim this river like fish for eternity. My lungs choke for air.

I see things. Visions? Hallucinations? Whatever they are, they're nightmarish. *Jennifer Regent standing on a mound of dead supernaturals, among them Trent and Teresa. Mom and Dad, being shot execution-style by the SSA. Fahaian becoming engulfed in the flames that he usually controls.*

William and Michi in a passionate clinch, turning their faces to laugh at me while they do it. The wendigo stuffing me down his throat.

My heart skips. I gasp, only to ingest a lungful of rancid River Styx water. I'm drowning. *I'm dying ... my last visage will be my friends dead or betraying me in the worst way possible ...*

An arm plunges into the water and clutches to the scruff of my neck, yanking me out. My lungs force out the water I've breathed in, leaving me a shuddering, coughing wreck. I feel weakened, even more than I've been since I descended into this place. My lungs continue to expel water, forcing it out of my mouth and nose.

I'm barely aware of someone helping to pat my back as I cough up more water. Trying to catch my breath, despite the swimming-pool sensation running through my entire head, I look over and find that it's Abaster, a very concerned expression on his face.

"Am I ... going to die?"

He smiles gently. "Not this day, Alanna. Not for lack of trying, though. It's okay, just get it out."

I cough loudly, which turns into a gurgle, and what feels like another three gallons of water spew from my mouth. I'm really nauseous now, and I need to get my equilibrium back, so I simply sit back in the boat and try to steady my head with my eyes closed. I can still feel Styx waters gurgling in my lungs as the sound of the boat's hull scraping the opposite shore comes to us.

"All right, get out of my boat!" Phlegyas is nearly swatting us out of the vessel with his oar. "I've got more assholes to pick up and too little time to do it."

We scramble out of the boat and onto the muddy shoreline. Phlegyas seems a little too much in a hurry to get back across once more, as he's fully pushed off and paddling away by the time we're able to turn around to see him. Abaster sighs deeply. "Please forgive him, Alanna. He's raging from an ancient hurt."

"Maybe so, but he could be a little nicer."

"You must try to understand, he deals with all of the worst sinners on a daily basis. He must be this brusque, because otherwise he would be rent limb from limb a million times a day. Come, though, our time with him is finished." He grasps my shoulders and turns me around to face an infinitely tall wall, one of several we have confronted thus far on our journey, glowing red with fire and reeking of death.

"Where are we?"

Abaster nods at my question. "Welcome to the City of Dis. Come, we must pass through the gates, and the guardians dislike the living."

I don't have to be told twice. As we approach the gates, I'm aware of several pairs of eyes glaring down on me from high above. When I look up, all I can see is gloom, though small, faint glints of red shine through it. As I grasp the handle of the entry gate, I hear screams from above, followed by the black streaks of demonic shadows diving down upon us.

"Living soul, halt! Those mortals who pass into this city remain for eternity, our playthings." The demons land hard around us, circling us. Each of them doesn't look quite as demonic as I would think … many still have human forms despite their bat-like wings. *"Show us who you are. You will be alone for eternity."*

My hand tightens on the Sword's hilt. Without thinking, I start to draw it, despite Abaster's cries. "No, stop! You, the fallen archangels, must recognize one sent by He Who Is Called I AM!"

They growl. None of them seem to care about what Abaster is telling them, so I guess it's my turn. I draw the Sword, the gauntlets clanking around my forearms. I spread my wings and twist my face into a scowl. *"I am the Guardsman, let me through!"*

"The Guardsman!" The scoffing of the demon before me catches me off-guard. *"Yet another symbol of the regard placed on humans above God's original chosen! You have no power here, Guardsman, you have only despair and defeat to look forward to."*

That tears it. Despite the thick mud my feet are being sucked into, I charge, flapping my wings to add power to my strokes. The Sword comes down through one of the demons, exploding him into a small dust storm. One tries to grab at a wing, but is met by the Sword slicing through his torso horizontally. I feel like I have infinite energy, but at the same time I fear for my level of power and my ability to continue on the journey if I continue at this pace.

I've defeated all but one of this party of fallen angels. The last one cowers before me, looking fearfully at the Sword's blade. *"I will let you in! Please don't destroy me!"*

The Sword slides securely into its scabbard. The cowardice shown by this demon is appalling. "See that you remember who it is that bested you today." My voice is still a growl. My energy level is nearly exhausted, and I'm running on pure adrenaline. My hands are shaking violently as the demon slinks past us and throws the gates open.

Abaster puts a hand on my shoulder. "Are you all right, Alanna?"

I nod, panting. "I will be." I reach for a bottle and slug down four large swallows of holy water. I've nearly emptied the first bottle, and that's both shocking and frightening because of my limited supply. Desperately trying to restore my energy level, I allow Abaster to lead me within the walls of Dis.

Chapter Sixteen: Dis

Day 6

The first thing that strikes me about the city of Dis is the noise level. Mostly ungodly screaming.

The sulfuric stench within the city walls is hard for me to handle, coming as it is from several open graves that dot the landscape. It's from these burning graves that I'm hearing the screams.

"What is going on here?" I demand of Abaster.

"The City of Dis is Circle 6. In this place, heretics burn in these graves, separated from their bodies until the true Day of Judgment when they will be reunited and sealed within these tombs forever." He motions with his stump. "Each of these holes contains a number of souls, all of whom committed the same or similar heretical sins. The worst of the lot burn with the highest intensity."

I scan the graves. I suppose I should have been doing this a while ago, but I start searching for Dad. I look into the burning graves, and the sights chill me. People stand shoulder-to-shoulder in the holes, lit afire, the red glow creating all the light in this place. The graves burn hotter than Pele's volcano, and much less cleanly. The distinct odor of burning flesh and hair permeates through the sulfur.

"Alastair Abaster! You come back here! I'm not doing this crap by myself for the rest of my life!" Another booming evangelist voice echoes from a distant grave, this one burning very intensely.

"Friend of yours?" I ask.

"Unfortunately. I spent time in that particular grave." He motions me over to where the grave is dug into the earth. "This particular tomb is for those who used the name of He Who Is Called I AM and defiled it for their own glory."

Just like you did, I finish in my head. "How many souls?"

"Innumerable. You must understand, Alanna, there is no particular time when corrupting the name of God was 'in vogue,' so to speak. There are sinners from time immemorial ... some of which were dispatched by Guardsmen themselves ... crammed into that grave."

I crouch down and bring my face as close to the flames as possible, looking toward a sinner wearing thick, dark glasses. "When did you come here?"

"By my reckoning, it was nearly a year ago. I've only seen your companion there for the last three months."

Something seems familiar about this soul, though I don't want to let on that I might know who he is. "What was your sin?"

"We used the Name of God to our own advantage. We blasphemed His Holy Name for our gain, for profit, for sex, for power. Now we burn here."

My eyes travel over to Abaster's stump arm. "Is this where that happened?"

Abaster nods. "I spent time in this very tomb, although my sins were varied and wide. I suffered torments in several levels of Hell. Only the worst of us sinners deals with that particular fate."

So you were a bastard before *Four Corners. Just great.* I return my gaze to the burning soul in the tomb. "I have been sent on a holy mission, to find an innocent soul. Did he come through here?"

The soul grinds what's left of his teeth. "You seek the betrayed Guardsman. I thought that Sword looked familiar ... yes, child, he came through here, but only briefly on his way to his final destination."

Dad was here! My heart swells, and my eyes get warm. "So he went further into the Inferno? How far?"

"How do you think I'll know this? I can't leave here, stupid!"

Suddenly this soul is very rude. I pull out the *Inferno* and flip open to the passages in Dis. "When Dante came through, he said you guys could see the future but were ignorant of the present. What do you see of the betrayed Guardsman's fate?"

The soul looks further down in the grave, until another soul wriggles his way to the surface. The features on this soul's face chill me instantly: another hellbound Sharpe. He narrows his eyes toward me.

"Sharpe daughter, know this. I have seen your future, yours and your father's. It is a future of pain and torment, of tears and sorrow. You will know despair like no one else has ever known. Joy will be nonexistent in your future."

My blood instantly chills. Is this what I have to look forward to if I rescue Dad? What if he means I won't rescue Dad? My tears are threatening.

"Ancestor, your warning is appreciated, but I must follow my fate wherever it leads, and I refuse to believe that my life to come will be despair and torment. I will find the wrongfully damned Sharpe, my father, and bring him home." I turn toward Abaster. "Let's go."

Abaster dips his face. "As you wish. Be forewarned, though, that this Circle is the easiest of the lowest levels of the Inferno."

My face is set. "I'll take that chance." Abaster carefully strides through the burning graves, and I follow his shadow. The holes of fire create an immense labyrinth throughout the city, and it's getting more and more difficult to follow my guide.

Maybe I should try another shortcut. I stretch out my wings. That's a mistake. The hot air from the graves creates a furious updraft which launches me high up in the skies of Hell. I narrow my eyes, straining to see what's ahead.

The most shocking thing I see from this high vantage point is the massive presence at the center of the place, imprisoned at the waist yet with his arms free to move about. Every once in a while I see him swat something on the ground. The remaining Circles stretch out toward him, caulking him within the ground, but not forming any kind of structure … I can't tell where one circle begins and another ends. All I can see is that they are nearly as large as the Circles I've already passed through.

I'm suddenly aware of a pair of glowing eyes piercing through me. The figure at the center.

Lucifer.

One of his hands stretches toward me. I flap hard to avoid a blow of unknown strength, because I don't want to be swatted back into one of the Circles I've already left. I strain and flap against the heated currents of air rising from the landscape, plunging myself toward the ground.

I see Abaster finally, standing at the edge of Dis, waving toward me. I strain hard against the waves of heat until my feet touch the ground once more. Quickly, I re-wrap myself in my wings.

"What did you see?"

I pant, trying to catch my breath. "The entire landscape … I saw all the circles … and the center …"

"Yes, so you have seen Lucifer. He does reside at the center of this place, forever imprisoned here by God. We must be cautious from here on in, Alanna, for the worst circles and the worst sinners are to come. Let us rest tonight, for you must prepare for the worst of the worst, and to do that you must acclimate."

I'm reluctant to do it, because I want out of this place as quickly as possible, but Abaster is convincing. We set up a camp and rest for the evening, at the start of which I finish off the first bottle of holy water. Sleep comes quickly as my tired muscles have no complaint when I relax.

Chapter Seventeen: Bestiary

Day 7

I feel surprisingly refreshed this morning, which is a good thing because I'm probably about to die.

When day breaks in Hell, it's not exactly like a pleasant sunrise in the real world. You only know it's morning when the screams intensify from the damned. It's this cacophony that awakens me; Abaster has kept watch all night, and as such is already up on his feet, waiting for me.

"Come, Alanna, we have far to go and not much time to travel. We must hasten your search."

My hand is already on the Sword's hilt at Abaster's words. He warned me yesterday that the remaining Circles would be harder to cross through, and I'm going to take him at his word on that. The tightening of my grip on the weapon is a comfort right now.

Abaster leads me deeper into the landscape of the Inferno, past the last of the burning graves of Dis, until we reach a varied landscape of red rivers, trees, and deserts. I can see across this area, and the torment of the sinners here is more palpable than those before.

"This is Circle 7, Alanna. The sinners here were guilty of the sin of violence."

That doesn't seem right. "Why aren't they swimming in the Styx with the wrathful?"

"There's different kinds of acts of violence, child, and not all of them require wrath. Some involve malicious intent, others self-loathing, and still others are violent but don't seem that way when being committed. Come, we must not delay … have your weapon ready, we will need it."

Uh oh. He hasn't warned me before about a fight forthcoming. This can't be good.

Nearly before that thought ends in my mind, I hear a bull's roar from a short distance away, followed by the thunderous trampling of hooves. Without thinking, the Sword comes out of its scabbard, and I'm ready for anything.

Except this. The creature stampeding toward me, looking to plow through me, has the torso of a man but the head and legs of a bull.

The Minotaur, of course. Why not?

The beast roars, as I watch Abaster shuffle his way quickly past the creature and into the Circle proper. It roars, stamps the ground, gnaws on its wrist, then charges. I flap my wings to get over the monster, barely tapping it on the back of the neck with the tip of the Sword. It crumples to the ground in a heap.

I sheathe the Sword, running to catch up with Abaster. "What just happened there?"

Abaster is smirking. "The holy power of the Sword is too much for the Minotaur. A simple touch was able to defeat it. Come, Alanna, that isn't the last of the dangers that will confront you."

I nod and continue to follow Abaster, even as the landscape shifts from solid earth to large, shifting rocks. Many of them have a hard time holding my weight, and start to shudder as I step on them. My wings remain slightly away from my body, in an attempt to keep my balance, but even this isn't enough sometimes when particularly large rocks underneath me shift and fall away.

"What happened here? Why is the land like this?"

Abaster shakes his head. "An earthquake. Millennia ago, an event occurred which rent Hell open and allowed many of the demons your family fought passage to Earth. What you're traversing here is the ruins of a great city which held those demons long ago. You must be cautious while traveling over this terrain, for much of the land is still unstable."

Well I can figure *that* one out on my own. I step on the wrong pile of pebbles and go sliding down a hillside, out of control, until I eventually roll within my wings to the hill's base. When my head stops spinning and I'm able to look up, I see that I'm at the feet of a horse.

Or part of one at least. Above the feet, glaring down at me, is a muscular man, attached at the waist to the horse's body.

Centaurs. Again, why am I surprised?

"Who are you, woman?" The timbre of lust vibrates in the beast's voice. As I come to my feet, I see there are other centaurs approaching from behind this one. A couple of them have sinister expressions on their faces, ones which scream rape.

"Stay back, all of you. I am on a holy errand!" I spread my wings to emphasize my words.

"You're still a woman. We haven't seen a living woman in many thousands of years." That same expression of lust is still on the lead centaur's face. I reach for the Sword, only to have my hand slapped away from the weapon by another beast who snuck up behind me. A third one is reaching for my other arm. A fourth has a grip on my wings.

They're picking me up. Oh God ...

I scream and writhe against the centaurs' clutches, but they're all horribly strong, all of them holding me fast. The lead one has his hands on my body, fondling me ...

William, I'm sorry ... I wanted it to be you ...

"Halt! All of you!" Abaster's commanding voice echoes toward the gang of rapists. They turn to the source, but the lead one only laughs.

"Alastair Abaster. We had our fun with you before, why do you come back for more?"

Abaster's face ... what's left of it, at least ... is angry. "I am Alanna Sharpe's guide through the Inferno. She has been sent on an errand by He Who Is Called I AM. You have no business with her."

The leader turns away from me to confront Abaster. "Listen here, damned soul, you cannot command us. What business of yours is it if we have this woman? We have gone without for far too long, it's only fair we should have our fun here!"

Abaster's voice is back in commanding mode. "Who said fairness was part of being in Hell? You're here for punishment, so you act as guards in this Circle! Leave her be, or it will be to your detriment!"

The other centaurs are confused and start to slacken their grip on me. That's all I need. My hand grabs the Sword and quickly draws it, closing the gauntlets around my forearms. Without thinking, I swing and behead two of the attackers trying to hold me down, reducing them to dust.

"You should have listened to Abaster, bastard!" I raise the Sword toward the gang leader, rushing with every intent to run him through.

"Enough!" A different voice booms through the air toward us, and is the only thing that stops me from making dog food out of the centaur gang leader. Another centaur, this one obviously much older and more respected, clops toward us. He makes a quick assessment of the situation, and then turns to the gang leader. "Pholus, are you disgracing your race once more?"

My breathing is fast. I level the Sword along Pholus's throat, making my intentions known. *Tell me who you are and why I shouldn't destroy Pholus where he stands. He tried to rape a Guardsman.*

The elder centaur narrows his eyes. "Is this true?"

"Lord Chiron, we have had no females for centuries, millennia, eons. Please let me have this one."

Chiron comes up to Pholus and slaps him across the face. "You damned fool, Pholus. This isn't just a woman, this is a Guardsman. See her weapon?" He points toward the Sword, still dripping with the blood of the two destroyed centaurs. "One swing of this weapon and you are done for. You've caused the destruction of your brethren. Go!"

Pholus looks downcast as he obeys his elder, turning away from us and trotting away. Soon the others join him, leaving just me, Abaster, and Chiron at the site.

"Abaster, don't think you're being allowed off the hook. What are you doing with a living Guardsman here?"

I don't think Chiron is going to be much of a threat, so I sheathe the Sword finally. My head spins, but I do my best to hide it. "He is my guide, Lord Chiron. I come on a holy errand, to seek the soul of a Guardsman imprisoned wrongly in the Inferno. Please allow this task to continue."

Chiron levels his eyes toward me. *Maybe I shouldn't have sheathed the Sword so soon.* The expression in his eyes, though, is not lust like Pholus but more understanding. "I see. I have seen this soul you seek, the soul of Cole Sharpe. He passed through here not a week ago, going further into the Inferno. I fear you will not find him here in this Circle, lady Alanna, but you may pass through here. I will assist you as much as I am allowed to."

I bow to Chiron. "Thank you, sir. I will remember you fondly to the world of the living."

Chiron actually cracks the first smile I've seen since I've been in Hell. "I appreciate that." He motions toward a different group of centaurs, from which one approaches. "Nessus is my right-hand assistant, lady Alanna, and as such he will guide you."

Nessus bows toward us. "Please, come with me. You must ride my back, for we centaurs are the only ones who can ford the river."

I don't want to fly much more here, as it seems to sap more strength than usual. I climb up on Nessus' flank, with Abaster behind me. The centaur rears briefly before breaking into a run toward a suspiciously red, bubbling river.

"We're crossing through the souls of those violent against property and other people. Vandals, fighters, and murderers are in this river."

The temperature's rising. "What's up with this river?"

Nessus answers me, although his voice shows his pain. "This is a river of boiling blood. As the sinners submerged here have drawn blood in the world of the living, so now do they reap the fruit of their violent acts now."

Abaster leans forward. "This is not limited to people being directly violent, either. Look out there."

I narrow my eyes and spy some of the souls being boiled alive in the river. Many of them have had the flesh boiled from their faces, and so are only identifiable by other features. Two skulls in particular draw my attention, one bearing a two-colored long beard and another with a toothbrush mustache.

I know these souls ...

Another soul bubbles to the surface and screams. "ALANNA SHARPE, YOU BITCH!"

My heart jumps in my throat, because I know that voice. I turn in the direction it came from, and see her. A recent arrival, since she still has most of her skin, though it's blistered and raw. A gaping hole which is filling in with more and more of the river's boiling contents.

Yolanda French.

"She cannot hurt you, Alanna, so pay her no mind." Abaster's words in my ear are slightly reassuring, but I'm still tense as she swims through the boiling river toward us.

How can I deal with this? I guess I have to confront her.

"You are here by your own acts, Yolanda. Your acts of violence against supernaturals left you here. I'm sorry you died the way you did, but you can't blame me for your punishment."

She grits her scalded teeth. "I can't blame you, but I can still KILL YOU!" Her arm rises out of the blood, revealing a gun arm.

Good God, she still has her powers here!

My hand is on the Sword, but when Yolanda's gun fires, instead of shooting a bullet it rips her entire arm off of her body. She screams in pain, only stopped short by Nessus's back hoof making contact with her face and knocking her back down into the blood. My heart races, but I know I'm safe now, and Abaster was right. She really couldn't hurt me.

An advantage of being a Guardsman in Hell.

Nessus reaches the opposite shore of the boiling river shortly after our encounter with Yolanda. He shakes off some of the blood, and then urges us to dismount him.

"This is where I leave you. Continue to the south, you will reach your destination." Nessus turns to me. "Chiron wishes you the best of fortune in your search for your father, lady Alanna." He bows to us before turning back and crossing the river once again.

Chapter Eighteen: Mother

Day 7, continued

Abaster motions ahead of us. "We must cross through the forest. Do not worry, your father is nowhere to be found in this wilderness."

That's good to know, because this place is the closest I've seen to a haunted forest thus far in this adventure. I can barely see through the thick stands of trees that now confront me, a startlingly different landscape from the ruins and the blood river we just left. I've felt safer in battles with the New Empire than I feel right now … and that's saying something since I've crossed through so much of Hell already.

My hand is on the Sword. It hasn't left the hilt since before we mounted Nessus. Abaster notices my apprehension and approaches me. "Are you all right, Alanna?"

I nod. "I will be. Once we're out of here, I'll feel better."

Abaster sighs deeply. "I'm not sure if you will, my girl."

Then I hear the screams. Clearly not human screams, though, and they circle over our heads. I look up and see what appear to be massive birds, like vultures, circling overhead.

The heads look wrong, though …

"What is this place?" My free hand is now clutching one of the remaining two bottles of holy water.

"This is the middle ring of Circle 7, a place where those who committed violence against themselves are sentenced to."

Violence against themselves? I take a closer look at one of the trees, as we pass by it. It's gnarled and twisted, but in the crook of two branches I can see a face, deformed and embedded within the tree's bark.

"These are souls, aren't they?"

Almost in answer to my question, one of the birds swoops down and rips a chunk off of one of the trees. A different kind of scream emerges, more human and agony than demonic. The bird settles on the ground and gnaws insistently at the lump of tree it has ripped off. When we approach closer, it becomes apparent that this is no bird … certainly it has a bird's body, but the head is that of a decrepit old woman. It's a harpy.

I look up at the others circling. Eight pairs of old woman eyes glare down at me. They swoop toward me, threateningly. I cover my head and duck, anticipating an attack.

One of them speaks, in an old-crone croak that's barely audible over the ambient screams of Hell. "Don't be silly, girl. We're not interested in you."

I look up. One of the harpies is standing right in front of me, her wrinkly face curled up in what passes for a smile, but looks more like a sneer. I clear my throat. "Why not?"

"Too alive. Why would we want to eat one of the living, when the dead are so much more plentiful … and to tell the truth, they taste much better, too!" The harpy cackles, and I'm struck by how similar her laugh is to the stereotypical "wicked witch" I always think of around Halloween.

Well, this harpy's friendly enough. "My guide mentioned this place is for those who committed violence against themselves. What does he mean by this?"

The harpy cocks her head sideways. "What do you think it sounds like, girl? Suicide, of course." She motions with one of her wings. "Every soul you see here had life on Earth and chose to end it themselves, rather than face the troubles and dangers of life. They squandered the greatest gift anyone is ever given, and as their punishment they remain motionless while we visit destruction upon them, much as they did to themselves in life."

I look over to the tree that had a chunk taken out of it, and notice that the spot missing bark appears to have flesh filling the hole … raw, bleeding flesh. Almost like the person was within the tree …

"You look very familiar to me, girl …" The harpy is stroking her chin with one of her wings thoughtfully. "You sure you haven't been here before?"

I nod. "I'm very sure. You wouldn't know me."

Another harpy yells over toward us. "How'd she get out of her tree?"

The harpy closes to us turns to her friend. "I know, right? It's weird. She looks just like her!"

My spine chills. Who do I remind these monsters of? "Tell me what you mean!"

Abaster takes my arm gently. "Maybe we should move on …"

The harpy near us cackles again. "Come on, dead soul, let the girl see it. Follow me." She flaps her wings and flies low down the path we were walking on. I work my arm out of Abaster's grip and run to keep pace. After what feels like miles, the bird-woman finally alights and lands in front of a particularly gnarled tree.

I look up at the same crook where on the other trees a human face was visible, and my heart jumps into my throat.

It's Mom.

My breathing starts coming fast. *Am I too late? Is Mom already dead?* I think I start whimpering, because the harpy taps me on the leg with her wing. "What's wrong, girlie?"

I bite my fingertips. "This is my mother … why are you showing me this?!" Tears are starting to fall down my cheeks again. "She can't be dead!"

Sadness and anger consumes me. I'm irrational. I draw the Sword and take a wild swing at the tree. *"Damn it, NO!"*

The harpy looks up at me with a confused expression. "Who ever said she was dead, chickie? I just said you looked like this tree, that's all."

I'm very confused. I look up at the tree, at the point where the Sword made contact. A long slash from what would be Mom's shoulder to just below her right breast has been cleaved in the bark, but there's nothing underneath it.

An empty tree?

I sheathe the Sword, trying to return to my rational senses. "Why is this tree even here, if there's no soul in it? Why was Ariel Sharpe headed for Hell?"

The harpy smirks, just as Abaster finally catches up to us. "Little girl, are you that naïve? This is a place for suicides."

"I can confirm that," Abaster adds, huffing and out of breath. "Your mother had one suicide attempt that I knew of, in her college days. It's possible that this tree appeared after that first attempt."

I look back up at the damaged, empty tree. Mom's face, clear as it can be, embedded in the bark … it's twisted into a tormented expression. The harpy, on the other hand, is far more interested in the Sword.

"What's this? A Guardsman, here?" Her eyes suddenly turn murderous. "You denied us this soul! Not only once, you denied us three times the soul of Ariel Vibria!"

I flap my wings as I jump backward from the lunge the harpy takes toward me. I don't want to fight her … she's doing her job, after all, but I also don't want to be killed before finding Dad. I draw the Sword again.

"What business do you have attacking a Guardsman, harpy? Stand down!" The Sword remains at *en garde,* but I keep backing off.

"The Guardsman prevented us from having this soul … denied us the sweetest soul meat we ever wished for!" The harpy lunges again. "Thrice she tried to take her life, and thrice a Guardsman came to her to turn her back from Hell's gates! Thrice she was told to remain, to await love that would save a life!"

My heart drops. I'm going to have to fight this beast. I swing the Sword toward her, only to have her duck away from the stroke. *"Her love did save a life, saved many lives! She saved the world!"*

The harpy roars. "She brought a Guardsman back from the dead! She denied Lord Abaddon his victory! The Guardsman is an abomination!" She lunges her head forward again. I swing the Sword at just the right time, catching her neck with the blade and cleanly lopping off the creature's head.

I turn and sheathe the Sword in one smooth motion as the harpy's body dissolves into dust. Her head continues to screech as it lands in the dust. "Die, Guardsman! Your victory is short lived!" A croak later, the head dissolves into dust like the body did.

I'm panting harder than I ever have in my life. I almost feel like I can't catch my breath. Abaster is right next to me, supporting me under one arm. "Are you all right?"

I nod. "What she said ... is that ... is it true?"

Abaster's face darkens. "I only know of one time. She may have tried two others, I'm not sure. I saw her after the first one ... we prayed together and I helped her overcome her desperation."

I look up at the guide, with what I'm sure are eyes filled with tears. "Is this ... is what I'm doing ... all going to be a waste? Will I save Mom?"

Abaster lowers his eyes. "Alanna, please, don't ask this ..."

I growl at the man. "I need to know, Abaster! Dante claimed souls here could see the future. Am I going to save Mom or not?" My hands clutch the lapels of what's left of his coat. "Answer me!"

Abaster sighs then looks straight in my eyes. "It's difficult to say, Alanna. When I see the future, I see death, destruction ... I don't see victory, but I don't see defeat either ... just human life lost and sadness. I can't see your mother or your father ... or even you."

This can't be true. I have to save her. I'm going to save her. I'm going to save them both ...

The pressure is getting to me. It's all I can do to crumble into a ball and weep.

I was right. This is *too much to ask of me.*

Chapter Nineteen: Violence

Day 8

The night passes without further incident in this part of Circle 7. No harpy attacks, no further weirdness. It's good on a physical level.

Mentally, however … I think I'm going insane the longer I stay down here. Every day, new horrors rise to meet me. I've been very strong up until now, but I feel that strength faltering. My hands shake now. My eyes have trouble focusing when I awaken. I don't feel like I can take a deep breath. My heart constantly races.

It might be related, but I haven't consumed any more holy water since Circle 6's camp. Gabe did warn me about this.

I reach behind me for one of the two remaining bottles, and my heart skips a beat for a moment as my hands find nothing. Eventually, though, they come to rest on one of the bottles. It's strangely heavy, though, and I'm having trouble bringing it to my mouth to drink.

What if it's been stolen … replaced with Hell water?

Disturbing thoughts aside, I bring up my hand, and can barely get the cap off.

Maybe I'm just way weak. I did *draw the Sword three times without taking a sip.*

I can only bow my head down to the bottle's neck, reaching my tongue out to the water and lapping it like a cat. The instant it touches my parched mouth, my strength starts to return … my physical strength, at least.

I'm still not quite up to speed in my mind.

I'm finally lifting the bottle to take a more satisfying sip when the first drop of rain lands on my hand and burns it. The sizzling sound and the pain alert me to something being amiss. I quickly cap the bottle and run for cover, which Abaster has already found.

"What's happening?" The rain starts to pour harder, and as it does I can watch it turning the ground to glass.

"Burning rain ... we're approaching this Circle's last ring, and we must be cautious."

I flip open the *Inferno* and find where we currently are. I read the passages carefully. "Fire rain?"

Abaster nods. "More like acid rain, but Dante didn't have the words for it. It burns everything and everyone it touches. We must be cautious, not only directly for your well-being but also for your supplies."

I understand instantly what he means. The bottles have to be shielded. Abaster removes what's left of his jacket and wraps the bottles up in it.

"Will that be enough?"

He nods. "Hopefully. I have no need for an Armani suit anymore, anyway." He looks up in the sky as the rain starts to diminish. "We might be all right to move, it's lightening up. Come, we must hurry, this rain falls throughout this ring."

We step out from under cover. A couple more drops hit me and they burn, but I quickly brush them off of my arms and shoulders, keeping up with Abaster. "Who do we find in this ring?"

"All those within this ring committed violence against God, living lives of weakness or defiance. Of course, there are multiple means of doing this, as you'll see."

As Abaster leads me along, I can only ponder that he must have spent time here ... after all, summoning a demon, being an Invader, and killing a Guardsman is pretty violent against God. So it comes as no surprise to him or me when a giant appears on the horizon, reaching his hands to the sky and screaming various obscenities.

Then the giant looks our way, and I want to hide. He smiles over at us. His voice booms. "Alastair Abaster! Come, join me, fight the power!"

Abaster smirks. "Much as I would love to, Capaneus, I must be moving forward. My companion needs to continue on her way."

Capaneus narrows his eyes as he looks at me. "Well well, another defiant soul! Join me here, girl. We will never let this break us! Fight on!"

My expression hardens as I regard the giant man, standing naked on the sand, covered in burn marks from where the acid has torn at his flesh. "For what reason do you rage? What reason have you to defy your punishment?"

That's surprisingly Biblical of me to say!

Capaneus only laughs. "Young girl, you have no idea. Defiance is its own reward! I defied armies in life, defied any power greater than my own, and now I defy the authority of this damned place to punish me!"

Now I'm angry. I quickly flap my wings and take to the air, alighting next to Capaneus' face, and kick him in the eye. "Then you're a damned fool, sinner, and you deserve whatever punishment you defy here! Defiance with no purpose is useless … only if your cause is right can defiance ever be right!" I call down to Abaster. "Let's leave this idiot to his raging!"

Capaneus looks hurt, but I don't care right now. I've got a father to save, and I have no time for ridiculous resistance with no reasoning. When I alight and land next to Abaster, he places his one hand on my shoulder.

"Well played, Alanna. Come, let us continue."

All too willing to leave the giant behind, I follow close to Abaster, noticing all of the souls who lie on the ground, partially buried in the sand. Many of them appear to be missing body parts, apparently eaten away from the rain. None of them are nearly as defiant as Capaneus.

"Who are these?" I ask.

Abaster nods. "The souls in this ring were blasphemers, directly violent against God. Many were false prophets, others simply defied their faith's teachings. They lie here and are burned from all sides … from the sand below and the rain above."

Just as Abaster finishes this, another brief squall starts falling, and more acid droplets pound against us. This time, however, there's no cover. The burning is annoying, but doesn't seem dangerous … it itches more than hurts at this point. I do, however, feel myself dragging, and once the rain passes I take another swallow from my holy water stock.

Will I need more as I go deeper?

As the system passes, I see Abaster moving at a quicker pace, as the landscape starts to change. Now the territory looks more trampled, but still scarred from the acid rains. Abaster suddenly pushes me backward as a soul trudges toward us … I'm glad that he does, as a small cloud continuously pours acid down on … it? Him? Her? I can't tell, the soul is so damaged.

"What is going on?" I hate asking all the time, but I need to know. Thankfully, Abaster doesn't seem to mind answering all the time.

"This ring is for those who were violent against nature. Those who tried to twist nature to serve their purposes, or damaged nature carelessly, are cast here to always feel the bite of the burning rains, no matter where they may tread."

Six more souls pass us by, all burned beyond recognition. All six are trailed by their own personal clouds, though some of them are different in appearance. Some look like regular storm clouds, but others look like exhaust, smoke, poison gas …

Pollution.

What's worse, it *smells* like pollution. I'd kind of hoped the really bad smells were behind us, but I guess since this is Hell, no such luck there. I run across the path back to Abaster's side before another group passes through. We walk a different path, away from these sinners, until we reach a ravine filled with red, bloody water.

"There's another guardian we must pass by in order to get to the next Circle. I will summon him here. You should continue into the rest of the ring, because your father may have come through."

It's a good idea. I can ask around. I move away from Abaster and make my way toward a similar desert landscape, not quite as burned by the rains. There are more souls trudging through this landscape, more of them being tormented, although their punishment seems to mainly be lying face down, weighed down by large crests.

I gasp when I see one I recognize … one of these souls is a Sharpe. I remember clearly when Dad shared with me his family history book, especially when we got to the pages with the family's crest.

"Daddy, what's that?"

"It's our family's symbol, Alanna. You know what a coat of arms is?"

"We just talked about it in school. Is this ours?"

"It is. See here? That's the Sword. And the stripes represent our bloodline's history throughout the ages … the red for the Crusades, the blue for Rome."

"What's this on the scroll?"

"Our family's motto. Ut Dei miles resurrectionis fortis contra infernum."

"What does that mean, Daddy?"

"It means, 'As God's soldier I rise, strong in the face of Hell.'"

The motto is what I need to be now … strong in the face of Hell. What strikes me about this hellbound Sharpe, however, is that the crest has no Sword in it … in fact, it appears the crest was vandalized to remove it. The motto has been changed, too, scrawled with a new one in its place: *Licet mihi succubuerit Satanae tabernus aeternaliter.*

I crouch down to see the soul's face. "What did you do in life, soul?"

The soul barely acknowledges my presence. He turns his head, eyes glazed over. Clearly he has been trapped in this position for far too long. Only one word creaks out of his mouth.

"Swoooooooooooooooorrrrrrrd …"

At least this soul doesn't seem nearly as dangerous as Ursus did. I simply back away from him. "Whatever you did in life, you had your time to be the Guardsman, and it's obvious you squandered it. Live your punishment, ancestor."

The soul looks like he's about to cry. I don't care … he's being punished, he deserves to be here. Only two Sharpes in Hell don't deserve to be here, and I'm looking for the other one. I turn on my heel back toward where Abaster stands.

"Alanna, we're just about ready." Abaster waves toward me.

I quickly return to his side. "Do you know Latin, by any chance? I found another Sharpe among those souls over there, and he had the family motto altered around his neck …"

"Not surprising," Abaster interrupts. "Those souls are the usurers, those who in life were violent against art. In our time, we call them 'censors.'"

So this Sharpe tried to censor art? Why? Just because he didn't agree with it? I shake off my doubts and continue. "He had our family crest, but the motto was changed to *'Licet mihi succubuerit Satanae tabernus aeternaliter.'* What does that mean?"

Abaster puts his chin in his remaining hand, until his eyes spring open. "Certainly not a family motto to be proud of, that's for sure. Roughly, it means 'May I lie forever under Satan's boot.'" I don't have time to react to the perversion of my family's symbols before a massive creature rises out of the ravine we passed by earlier, a mismatched monster with a man's face, serpent's body, and furry paws.

"What the hell?!"

Abaster puts his hand on my shoulder. "Take it easy, Alanna, this is the next guardian. He has agreed to allow us passage into Circle 8. Alanna, this is Geryon."

Geryon smiles a snaggletoothed grin at me. *"Truly an honor to meet Guardsman. Not much time, though. Must continue on."*

Can't argue with that much. I collect Abaster into my arms and flap my way up to Geryon's face. "How do we reach Circle 8?"

Geryon grins wider. *"Take you. Fast flight."* He reaches out with one of his paws and grabs us. I shriek as he squeezes the breath out of me, then feel my stomach lurch as he takes off nearly straight up at top speed. No sooner has my stomach dropped into my butt, it flies up into my throat as the beast begins a descent just as violent as the beginning of the flight.

When he lands, Geryon opens up his paw and drops us roughly on rocky terrain. I feel like I punctured a lung in the trip, but I can't disagree with the beast, it certainly was a fast flight.

Abaster waves toward the monster. "Thank you, friend!"

Geryon waves child-like at us. *"Happy you see me!"* He takes off again, I would assume headed back to his own Circle.

Abaster turns his attention back to me. "Are you all right, Alanna?"

I cough and a little bit of blood jumps into my mouth. Suitable, I have to suffer violence to leave the Circle of the violent. I wipe the blood away with my hand, trying to hide it from my escort. "I'm all right, considering."

"Good. We must keep moving. Circle 8 awaits us."

Chapter Twenty: Broken Bridges

Day 8, continued

My head swims slightly. My breathing is slightly ragged. Even a sip of holy water isn't helping me … I think I'm dying.

Abaster is insistent, though, that we have to continue into Circle 8. My ribs are killing me … no doubt that Geryon must have cracked one or two … and I'm still coughing up a little bit of blood.

Think of Dad, girl.

Trying to think about Dad keeps me moving forward, even as my body wants me to drop. I finally reach Abaster's position, standing at the edge of the first of a series of canyons.

God, what I wouldn't give to glide through my canyon once more …

"Pay attention, Alanna." Abaster's admonition slaps me quickly out of reverie, which must have been obvious because he seems annoyed. "Circle 8 is where those sinners guilty of simple fraud are punished for eternity. We need to cross through this Circle carefully, because everywhere there are deceivers and the dishonest."

My eyes focus on several broken structures hanging over the canyons. "Is there any way to cross without entering these?"

Abaster shakes his head sadly. "In Dante's time, the bridge over the sixth Malebolgia was the only one that was broken. A short time ago, something else broke all of the others, so we will need to pass through all of them." He puts a hand on my shoulder again. "Brace yourself, because this only gets worse from here."

I nod in agreement and take another sip of the holy water, hoping it starts healing me soon. I hold up the bottle and check its level: I've drunk a third of the second bottle.

I'm not going to have enough to get to the end ...

I spread my wings and try to ignore the stabbing pain in my side as I do. "This will be the fastest way. Let's go."

Abaster lifts his arms up, allowing me to pick him up by his armpits, and I leap into a dive into the first Malebolgia. The sight that greets me as we enter, though ... lines and lines of sinners, dressed in rags if even dressed, marching in opposing lines and being continuously whipped. The smaller demons that torment these sinners are almost comical in their appearance ... considering the descriptions Mom and Dad gave me of the demons *they've* fought, these ones almost seem like stereotype devils.

"These sinners are those who used sex to commit fraud. The eastbound line contains the pimps and panderers, who profited from forcing sex on those weaker than themselves." Abaster points his stump toward the line approaching us. "The westbound line contains the seducers."

A demon looks up at us when it hears Abaster's voice, and swings its whip at us. "Alastair Abaster! We're not finished here! Reclaim your place in this line, seducing bastard!"

The demon swings the whip again, and this time he strikes us both. The pain stings like a thousand hornets, and it brings me crashing down to the ground, allowing Abaster to roll away from me as I find myself at the feet of the seducers. At once, they all start after me, and I'm suddenly reminded of the centaurs in Circle 7 ...

The Sword is quickly out, tight in my gauntleted grip.

"Back off! I am not your plaything!"

"Back in line!" A small demon runs up next to me and whips its charges back into the marching line. It looks up at me and grins, sharp, jagged teeth forming a bear trap of a face. "You are Alanna Sharpe, the Guardsman, are you not? You have Vibria blood, am I right?"

My heart thrums in my chest. *"What business is that of yours?"*

The dragon roar that is my voice with the Sword drawn doesn't seem to faze the little demon. "Tell Julian we can't wait to whip his ass!" It giggles incessantly, only stopping when I cleave it in half lengthwise with the Sword, screaming.

Julian can't be damned ... he can't be ...

Tears are starting to fall, but I only notice when I finally sheathe the Sword. Abaster has sped his way over to me.

"Tell me, Abaster ... is this where my grandfather's going to wind up?"

"Alanna, please, we must keep moving ..."

I yank Abaster closer by his remaining arm. "I need to know *now!*"

His face grows dark and sad again. "The westbound line, the seducers ... these are all men and women who abandoned their committed lovers when it was convenient for them. Your grandfather left Shanee behind after a night of passion, alone to raise her daughter. I'm sorry, Alanna."

This is devastating news to me. Julian's a sweet old man ... he regrets his actions enough, he doesn't deserve this!

Think of Dad, girl. You need to keep moving.

I wipe my eyes, grab Abaster, and take back to the air. None of the other small demons notice. The air is heavy and hard to flap through, and it just seems to keep getting heavier the further down into Hell I go, but we finally breach the crest of the first Malebolgia. Truthfully, though, that's nothing compared to what awaits in the second, which I can already sense by the smell.

Great, another load-of-crap part of this place. What's with the obsession with dung around here?!

"Abaster, is there any place I can set us down to camp that doesn't drop us into that toilet below?"

He looks up at me, and his words are almost blown away. "Not really, not unless we can cross through and get to the third Malebolgia. We'll need to suffer through the flatterers, though!"

I roll my eyes, dropping us down into the stinky cavern. The souls trudging through, coated head-to-toe in filth, look up pleadingly at us, reeking and spewing more of the crap out of their mouths.

Hold it in, Alanna. Think of Dad.

I choke back my nausea to talk to Abaster. "Why did you call these people the flatterers?"

"They gave untrue compliments to gain favors in life. Since for all intents and purposes they spoke excrement, they are doomed to wallow in it for eternity."

Gurgling in my stomach is making me want to accelerate. I flap my wings harder, fighting the heavy air to get myself and my payload out of this place. We finally reach the top and without slowing down begin our descent into the third Malebolgia.

We happen to be close to the bridge that should have crossed this cavern, and I have an opportunity to look at the damage. It's cleanly broken at two places. This isn't usage damage.

This bridge was chopped down.

Fortunately, there's no filth, no stench, or anything remotely resembling a bodily emission in this Malebolgia. All there seems to be is a hole with a pair of feet sticking out of it, being set on fire. I alight and set Abaster down next to the hole, only to watch him collapse in agony.

I'm immediately at my guide's side. "What's wrong?" This is the first discomfort I've seen him in this whole time.

He rubs his feet with his one remaining arm. "I'm feeling my punishment here, that's all. It's my burden to bear, Alanna, please don't concern yourself with it."

"Well, sorry, but I *am* concerned with it because without you as my guide I'm screwed! Tell me what's going on, please?"

Abaster drops his face slightly. "We're in the Malebolgia that punishes simony."

That explains a lot. "I don't know what that is. Should I?"

"It's not a common thing in our time, so I'm not surprised you don't know. Simony is the buying and selling of church positions and spiritual favors. It's basically profiteering from religion."

I smirk. "Let me guess … you spent time down in that hole, didn't you?"

Abaster rubs his feet harder. "This was the place I was when I was summoned to guide you, Alanna. This is my most recent punishment, for one of the more egregious sins I committed, building a fortune on the shoulders of my church."

I look down at Abaster's feet, realizing I really hadn't noticed them up until now, and notice that he's not wearing shoes. More than that, I also notice that his feet are smoking. I turn back to the hole. Sure enough, whoever the soul is at the top of the hole is barefoot, the skin blackening and crisping in the flames engulfing them.

I crouch down next to the feet. "Hot enough down there?"

A booming voice comes up from deep in the hole. "Back off, bitch! We've been cooking in here for centuries, let us suffer in silence!"

I'm suddenly feeling very vindictive. I have no idea why. I'm smiling like a maniac as I call back down the hole. "Why did you do what you did in life? Why did you try to profit from your religion?"

More grumbling. Growls. *Why am I enjoying this?*

I'm about to send another rejoinder down when I feel myself being pulled back by Abaster, who forces the mouth of the open holy water bottle between my lips. I suck down a choking swallow. "Gah, what the hell? What are you doing?!"

Abaster looks grim. "Saving your soul, Alanna. Don't turn into one of these keepers of Hell while you're here. It's not your duty."

My head starts clearing, and my jovial mood is going away. Now I realize what I've been doing … verbally abusing those already damned … and I feel horrible about it.

I need to hurry. I've been down here too long.

Day 9

I stand on a barren plain, encircled by people I know. Friends, family, all people I love. Their faces glare at me accusingly.

The first words come weakly from my mouth, as I turn to face them all. "What have I done?"

"You abandoned us!" Michi's voice squeaks at me. "You left us alone, left us to face a world that hates us, a nation that wants us dead. Now we're in Hell because of you."

"You betrayed our trust," Uncle Cyrus booms. "We brought you to Avalon, we gave you every chance to accomplish your quest, and yet you squander our aid."

I'm starting to breathe faster. "I'm sorry … please forgive me …"

"Forgive you?" William's question is harsh and cold. "You climbed up on our shoulders, we held you up, we supported you, and now here you stand before us, changed, different … demonic. You disgust me."

My heart is breaking. My tears are falling faster. "I just want my family back …"

"Who says we want you *back?" The question comes from Mom, behind me. I turn to face her, and see her cradled in the arms of Dad …*

Wait, not Dad. It's Scolar.

"Mom … how could you …?"

Scolar sneers at me. "Your cowardly father can't compare to a true man, hatchling. I think your mother prefers the darker side of things ... wouldn't you agree?"

I try to rush Scolar, but discover that my elbows are locked in shackles, bolted to the floor. I'm helpless to watch him paw my mom ... but when he turns back toward me, his face has changed, to that bald bastard Gerard, the one who made me into a dragon and turned me crazy enough to wreck Chicago. He grins at me just like Scolar did, and motions toward Mom.

Only then do I notice that Mom is pregnant ...

I jump upright, screaming. *Just a dream. Only a dream. But it felt so damn real ...* I taste blood in my mouth and realize that I've been chewing on my lip while having this incredibly horrible dream. Abaster is next to me, crouching and showing his concern on his face.

"Are you all right? What happened?"

I swallow hard, some of the blood from my lip coating my tongue now. "It was just a dream ... but it was so real and so hurtful ..."

My face is buried in my hands, but I'm surprised to suddenly feel Abaster putting his arm around me, in as close to a hug as he can manage now. "I understand, Alanna. Try to hang in there, because your father's close, I know it. Your journey is nearly over."

I'm shaking, I'm weak ... even after taking a sip of the holy water, I'm still much weaker than I was at the start. I allow Abaster to help me to my feet, which it takes a moment for me to balance on. I check all of my supplies ... the Sword is still reliably at my side, the two bottles hooked securely to their belt ... and take a deep breath, which is hard to do in the stifling air of Hell. "Okay. Let's keep moving."

Abaster nods and motions to an opening in the sheer rock face of the Malebolgia. "This way, Alanna. We've got seven more bolge to get through before we're out of Circle 8."

I obediently fall in line behind my guide, allowing him to lead me through the tunnel to the next canyon. When we emerge, it's almost comical to observe the souls trapped here. They are all naked, and they trudge backward through a featureless landscape, mainly because their heads are literally on backwards.

This actually sounds familiar. I flip open the *Inferno* again. "Bolgia 4, the soothsayers."

"Indeed," Abaster confirms. "Because these souls chose to look too far ahead of their time, they are now forever doomed to look behind them. Sadly, this means that your father will not be here."

I look over at Abaster, maybe too angrily. "We've gone most of the way through this Godforsaken place, and have only seen brief wisps of clues as to where Dad went. How are we going to know where he is for sure?" I'm tapping my foot now. "You said you *knew* where he was. Why haven't we found him yet?"

Abaster sighs. "We need to follow his path. Unfortunately, it's a long one. We need to follow his footsteps to get to where he is. When I told you I knew where he was, I did not lie to you … it's just that I only *vaguely* know his location. He's in the ninth Circle."

I slap my forehead. "Then why in God's name couldn't you have *told* me that?"

The realization hits me, just as Abaster responds. "Because I was told *not* to."

Damn you, Gabe, this has you written all over it! What, getting tossed around Hell is your idea of a training exercise?!

I growl, impotently because I know it's not Abaster's fault really, but I just need to blow off some anger. "The next time I see the man who told you not to tell me, I'm going to kick his ass."

Abaster seems slightly bemused. "You're a far braver soul than I, Alanna. Come, we must continue if we're going to get to Circle 9, and we have far to go in this Circle."

I clutch the Sword tightly. Abaster notices this.

"You won't be needing that, hopefully, through the rest of this Circle. The demons here are uninterested in the living, and the dead are virtually helpless."

That assurance only makes me tighten my grip. "You'll forgive me if I'm a little overly cautious, won't you?"

Abaster nods. "Very well. Let's continue." He motions toward a wooden archway built into the opposite wall of the canyon. We make our way over to the place and through the doorway. I'm barely through it when Abaster throws his arm in front of me to stop me from walking. "Careful!"

I look down below my foot and discover why. The entire canyon is flooded with boiling tar. Souls are being dunked in it by flying black demons who cackle the whole time.

"This bolgia is for those souls guilty of graft and bribery. These souls either paid for political favors, or were in positions of power and took money for influence." Abaster crouches down and holds his hand above the tar. "This pitch is incredibly hot, Alanna, so be careful. We might have to fly over this."

One of the winged demons notices us. It grins. "Hey, it's our next customer! Alastair Abaster, get over here! We've got your hot tub all set up!" The demons laugh amongst themselves, continuing to dunk souls.

I spread my wings and step between Abaster and the laughter. "He's my guide right now. Once I'm done with him, you can do what you will, but for now he's mine!" I draw the Sword to emphasize the point. *"Now let us pass!"*

The demons don't stop laughing … what are they, flying hyenas? "Sure, sure … soon enough. We're patient." More laughter, even louder and more raucous.

Abaster jumps up on my back. "Thanks, Alanna. Let's fly."

I nod and flap my wings ... the Sword is still out, because I think I'll need the Guardsman's strength right now ... and lift off from the ground, reaching for the top of the bolgia. Fortunately, it's a short flight to clear the canyon wall and drop into the next pocket of torment, which seems populated by sluggish monks.

We alight and drop down next to one of the slow-moving shapes. Abaster slides down off of my back, as I sheathe the Sword finally. My head swims even more than it did before, and I take three large swallows of holy water.

The bottle's only got a third left, then I'm down to my last one. I have to make it last.

"This is where the hypocrites are punished," Abaster mentions. "The punishment is sewn into the clothing ... these cloaks weigh them down, so that they may not move quickly, nor ever be relieved of the weight of their sins."

I stroke my chin. "Why do they all look like monks?"

"Many of the men punished here were clergy, many of whom followed the 'do as I say, not as I do' doctrine." Abaster is pulling on his collar. Clearly he's nervous ... he might be awaiting punishment in this bolgia. Then again, he *is* awaiting punishment in the last one, too.

"May I speak to one of them?"

Abaster raises an eyebrow. "Certainly. As a matter of fact, there's one approaching that might be of interest to you. Let's let him arrive."

Four hours of waiting later, the hooded, cloaked monk-like figure finally reaches us and pauses. "Why are you here, living woman? And why do you torment me with that Sword?"

I'd like to pull back his hood, but it's way too heavy. "How do you know the Sword?"

"It was mine, during the war."

I crouch down to see this man's face, and discover that yes, he certainly is a Sharpe. A hellbound Sharpe, trudging through the afterlife in a lead-lined monk's cloak. "Which war?"

I see a smile. "The war between the brothers. I was General Grant's secret weapon."

An American Sharpe, from the Civil War no less. I'm dreading this ... "What was your sin that brought you here?"

He sighs. "I fought for the Union, and advocated for emancipation. At the same time, I held significant property in South Carolina, complete with a full staff of slaves. My mouth said 'free the slaves,' while my actions said 'let them die where they stand as long as I continue to profit.' For this great sin against humanity and against what the Sword stands for, I wear this robe of lead, made from the chains I held humanity in."

His breathing is heavy, with the obvious strain of standing with the robe around his shoulders. I'd better make this quick before he drops. "Did you see another Sharpe come through? A living soul?"

He looks up at me, which takes a superhuman effort on his part. "You know, poor old Isaiah did see something weird ..."

I smirk. "Are you Isaiah?"

He nods and smiles. "Isaiah Sharpe, at your service ... yes, I saw him, I saw my descendant as he passed through here. He had a big escort, though; six demons that I've never seen around these parts were shuffling him through awful fast."

Progress, finally! "Which way were they going?"

Isaiah lifts his hand slowly to point toward a door on the far wall. "Through there. On the express train to Circle 9, I think. He was fighting like crazy, though, like he didn't belong here."

That sounds like Dad, all right. "He doesn't belong here, that's why I'm here. I'm trying to bring him back." I clutch the Sword in my hand. "The Guardsman is here to rescue her predecessor."

Isaiah eyes me head to toe. "You, a Guardsman? You're barely old enough to be off the farm …"

"Maybe so, but the Sword is mine, and the duty is mine to bring my father home." I look up at the mouth of the bolgia, toward the wrecked bridge. "By the way, Isaiah, how long has that bridge been broken?"

He looks up and chuckles. "Oh, *that* bridge? It's been busted since the Crucifixion. Now the other bridges, that's a story there … they all were broken just after your daddy came through, girl. I actually saw who did it, too."

This has my attention. "Who?"

Isaiah looks back and forth, then leans closer to me. "Don't tell anyone it was me who told you … but I saw one of the lords of Hell pass through, and he had his daughter with him. Just after that, the rest of the bridges broke."

That chill in my spine is back. "Do you know the names of the demons?"

Isaiah nods. "It was Mammon, and his daughter's name is Mamuna. They were talking about something … something big going on back in America, actually, and how the bridges would 'make it too easy,' whatever that means. Mamuna was really animated about it, really."

I take a deep breath, and then gently kiss my ancestor on his forehead. "Thank you, Isaiah. I appreciate your help."

He grins widely. "Hey, if you don't mind my asking, who are you? How far down the bloodline are you?"

I smile and unfurl my wings. "My name's Alanna Sharpe, and I guess you're my great-great-great grandfather."

He smiles and nods and continues on his way. "Good luck, Alanna. If and when you find your father, give him my greetings." The trudging robe mass that is Isaiah Sharpe slowly walks away.

I turn to Abaster. "Mamuna has something to do with the New Empire, doesn't she?"

He shrugs. "I wouldn't know. Politics isn't my specialty … right now it's guiding you to your father. We should continue."

I nod in agreement, collecting my guide by his armpits and taking off. Somehow, the flight feels easier now … maybe because Isaiah's information gives me hope.

Fight them, Dad. Fight them until the end. I'm coming for you.

Chapter Twenty-One: Ice

Day 10

The rest of the Malebolgia are easy to pass through, thanks to Abaster's knowledge of who resides within each one, not to mention the ability to find passages in each one to the next. I just wish that there wasn't so much weirdness in each one.

Bolgia 7 made me cringe because I remember my fear of snakes from the rez. The sinners there, all thieves, were constantly being bitten by poisonous snakes, and as a result their identities were changing. With faces and voices and even genders constantly changing, it was difficult to talk to anyone, so we decided to continue onward. Bolgia 8, on the other hand, was too warm for my taste, as we made our way through a forest of flaming pillars.

Abaster informed me, with a shaky voice, that the souls being burned within each pillar were false advisors and counselors, all of whom had led others to downfall or death. Most of them did it maliciously. I have a feeling this is another garden spot awaiting its chunk of Abaster's flesh.

Hell can wait. Dad comes first.

It's not until we reach Bolgia 9 and begin wading in blood again that my hackles are raised and the Sword's hilt tightly gripped in my hand. "I thought you said we weren't going to run into any more trouble in this Circle!"

"I did, yes. And we won't. This is the blood of the schismatics, the sowers of discord, those who chose to create artificial divisions by claiming the hearts, minds, and souls of others." Abaster pulls on his collar.

"Another place waiting for you?"

He nods. "You don't create much more of a schism than I did. Besides, there's someone here who considers me an old friend …"

I don't know what he means by this, but then it's illustrated to me as a familiar-looking Sabre takes a chunk out of Abaster's shoulder. Instantly, I'm at *en garde,* the Sword clutched in both hands.

"Invader! I destroyed you!"

Standing directly behind Abaster, the familiar death's-head helmet, the dark metal armor, the blank, soulless eyes of the Invader evaluate me. *"Invader? I think you have me mistaken for someone else."*

The voice doesn't sound right. Maybe he's got a point ... but that's the Sabre! I can't possibly forget that weapon!

"How is it you wield a Sabre that has been destroyed?"

"This old thing?" He waggles the Sabre, and then sheathes it. To my surprise, the Invader's armor doesn't disappear. *"Oh, wait, I think I know what's going on here ... you're talking about Abaddon's shitty copy of my blade!"*

Abaddon's copy? There's more than one? My blood runs cold. *"I destroyed the Sabre in the world of the living. I seek its previous holder."*

"I don't think you do. I think you seek the man the previous holder's keeping hostage in the next ring over ... oh crap, I wasn't supposed to tell anybody about that!"

I sheathe the Sword. Obviously, this is no threat. "So let me get this straight ... the Sabre is just a copy of your sword?"

"You got it." He draws the blade again. *"I've been here hacking away at these scumbag sinners for eons, and my old reliable weapon hasn't failed yet.*

Abaddon was impressed, so he asked if he could model a weapon from it. He wound up making a crummy copy that he flung up to Earth to be wielded by a bunch of troublemakers." The eyes in the helmet narrow as the sword reaches toward Abaster's throat. *"Troublemakers like this douche here."*

I nod. "Exactly, and they've sported armor much like yours."

The demon rolls his eyes and sheathes his sword again. *"Abaddon, you dick! At least get creative with something, instead of just copying the best! Where is he, anyway?"*

I clear my throat. "Sorry ... my mom killed him a while ago."

There's a delay in reaction, but eventually the armored devil starts laughing hysterically.

This is a waste of time. "Will you allow us to pass? We have business in Circle 9."

He's still laughing, now he's doubled over. At least he has the decency to nod and motion us away from him. *"Hey, if you get a chance, find the last guy who had the copy and give him a wedgie, 'cause he probably deserves it too!"*

Oh, he's getting a lot more than that, believe me. I spread my wings and pick up Abaster again. I figure it'll be easier to cross through the final bolgia through the air rather than walking. As I take off, the armored demon collapses into more giggles, which doesn't stop him from pulling out his sword and lopping off another sinner's feet.

Abaster sighs. "What a strange demon."

For once, I have to agree with my guide. "Is it really that funny that mom killed Abaddon?"

Abaster looks up at me. "You might have noticed that many of the denizens of Hell are surprised you're here, that you would be the one taking the journey. It's because of your gender. They still don't tend to take women seriously here."

I smirk. "By any chance, would that include Mamuna?"

I feel my guide cringe at the mention of the demon's name. "Possibly. Her father is a prince here, but I've rarely heard of Mamuna herself even being allowed to leave the circle Mammon rules."

This is definitely food for thought as we glide over Bolgia 10 and observe the diseased souls below. I vaguely hear Abaster referring to the souls down below as counterfeiters and alchemists, but just seeing the pestilence and affliction that all of those souls are being punished with, a part of me is happy to be flying overhead for fear of possibly catching something contagious if we were to land.

Abaster motions toward the ledge of the bolgia. "Alight over there. We'll rest for the night."

I comply with my guide's instruction and set him down gently on the ground, right next to the edge. I scan around us, looking for any danger, and not seeing any I settle down on the ground. Abaster has long since sat down already.

"What's in the distance there?" I point toward what looks like two towers, in the misty distance.

"It's the entrance to your goal, to Circle 9. We're nearly there, but all the same it's going to take time to get to your father." He lies down in the dust.

I can't get that comfortable, not yet. "What will become of you? Once I get to Dad, what happens to you?"

Abaster smirks slightly. "I go back to the bolge I was in when I was contacted. I continue my punishment, which is only right for the great sins I committed in life."

I'm very confused. "So ... it seems like you're being passed from place to place, just because of the wide range of sins you committed. What happens when you reach the innermost Circle?"

I think tears are falling from Abaster's remaining eye. "I get sent back to Circle 2 and I get to experience the torments all over again. Eternally."

I sigh sadly. *Wait ... what? Why am I feeling sympathetic? This is Alastair Abaster, the man who killed Dad, who tried to destroy the world ... who betrayed Mom's trust ...*

"Why did you do it?"

Abaster seems confused by my question. "What do you mean?"

I look over toward him, eyes slightly glistening. "Why did you commit your sins in life? Why did you betray a holy trust given to you by your congregation and all those who felt you were important to them?"

Abaster's eye turns down. "Are you sure you want to know the answer?"

I nod. "I think I deserve to know."

"Really? What do you know of what you deserve?" Abaster sounds angry as he sits up and faces me. "What do you know of pain, of torment? What do you know of punishment? What do you know of reward? Nothing! What are you other than a scared little girl playing adult games?"

"I know that my mother placed her trust in you, long ago, and that was a trust you betrayed by trying to destroy the world and by killing her husband!" My voice is approaching the dragon's roar. "I've had both parents taken from me, I've had my home taken away ... for God's sake, I've had my damn *humanity* taken away from me! And you think I don't know PAIN AND TORMENT?!"

For the first time in Hell I feel the churning in my guts, and the flames rising up my throat. Before I can stop it, I'm firecasting and completely coating my guide in flames. I can see him flinching in the glow before the fire finally subsides. He's entirely coated in char: I can see his eye opening and looking through me. With a loud crack, his mouth opens to speak.

"You ask why I committed sin, betrayed your mother's trust? Here's your answer. I did it because I'm human, and at the time I sinned I only thought of myself, what advanced me, what gave me pleasure. And for that selfishness, I have doomed myself to an eternity of repeating tortures." He shakes his head and a layer of ash flies off of his face. "Do I regret it? You better believe I do. Can I do a damn thing about it? No. Therefore, there's no point in having this conversation."

My heart sinks. He's right. There really *isn't* any point, because whether he regrets it or not, he did the crimes and he'll have to pay for them. Forever.

What price will I pay for my actions?

I slink down to a horizontal position, clutching to myself. I feel incredibly cold right now. Tears are threatening, and despite my best efforts they fall.

William, Michi ... Mom, Dad ... at what cost do I save you all?

Day 11

Abaster wakes me roughly. "Come on, let's go. We need to move forward."

I try to shake the cobwebs out of my head, to no avail. My head's swimming. Maybe I shouldn't have tried to cook my guide last night, because the effort of producing fire is kicking my butt this morning. I try to reawaken myself with another swallow of holy water.

No effect. I swallow more, and more, until I finally feel my eyes clear up. I hold the bottle up in front of my face. Empty.

Now I'm frightened. I'm down to my last bottle of holy water, and the most dangerous level of Hell is approaching.

Fear and pessimism is overtaking me. *I'm not going to make it …*

"Stay with me, Alanna. Let's go."

Abaster's voice brings me back to the present. I discreetly discard the empty vessel as I stand up to join him. Once at his side, I feel like I have to say something about last night. "Hey, I'm sorry about the argument … about trying to burn you up. I shouldn't have done that. I overreacted, and I'm sorry about that."

He nods deeply. "It's my fault too. I know of your situation on Earth, Alanna, and I should have known of the torments you've lived through already." He takes my hand, very gently. "We are not very far from your father. We'll see him soon, I'm positive. You've come a very long way, especially for a mortal, and he should be very proud of the effort you've put forth thus far."

Somehow this makes me feel better. I smile gently. "Thank you … Alastair."

Now it's his turn to smile. It must mean a lot to him that I've put him on a first-name basis. "Let's continue."

I nod and allow him to lead me forth, away from the ledge of the final bolge of Circle 8. Those towers are looming ahead once more, making me a little nervous. They don't seem like the towers we saw earlier, guarding the city of Dis.

These seem more … alive.

"Circle 9 has several guardians," Abaster mentions. "We will need to convince one of them to allow us passage."

"What kind of guardians?" I always need to ask so I know what to expect.

He points forward. "You can see them actually."

I narrow my eyes, allowing the dragon's vision to come to me. As the view focuses, I see that those towers have faces at the top … wait, not faces, they're heads.

Giants. I've encountered every other fairy-tale nightmare down here, may as well get giants in too.

We quickly approach where the giants are standing, a massive well that Abaster mentions surrounds the entirety of Circle 9. I'm only now realizing the scale of this crossing as we stand at the edge of one of the wells, and are at the navel of one of the giants, this particular one carrying a large horn hanging around his neck. He turns his head to one side and lets out a massive yell of gibberish.

I open up the *Inferno* and flip pages until I find our location. "I'm guessing this is Nimrod?"

Abaster nods. "Indeed, one of the architects of the Tower of Babel. His punishment for his arrogance is twofold: he must stand guard as a giant at Circle 9, and his speech will never be coherent for the remainder of eternity." Abaster motions past the giant. "Come, we have to reach one of the giants who can let us through."

We begin pacing around the edge of the well, passing several giants who are on some way restrained. As we walk, Abaster tells me small details about each one of them. Ephialtes and Otus, the twins who thought they could challenge the gods by building a ladder out of mountains. Tityos, who attempted to rape Leto, the mother of Apollo and Artemis. Typhon, the father of all monsters who was defeated by Zeus himself, and his mate Echidna. Most imposing of all, we pass by the imprisoned Goliath, still sporting a massive dent between his eyes from where David's stone struck him.

We pass by a space with no giant. I turn to my guide, questioning. "What happened to the guardian here?"

Abaster turns and looks, then smiles. "Ah ... you mean Mahishasura. He's been gone for a long time, actually. He escaped to the living world when the earthquake struck, only to be defeated by the servant of the goddess Durga."

I thought the name sounded familiar! I can't help but smile. *Aunt Kitty destroyed one of the guardians of the ninth Circle of Hell. What a woman.*

"We're here. Antaeus! Come here!"

Abaster's call is met by another giant, this one unrestrained. He bends over and narrows his eyes. **"Alastair Abaster, what business do you have here?"**

Abaster looks unfazed. "We must have passage to Cocytus, friend. I escort a Guardsman on a mission from He Who Is Called I AM."

Antaeus turns his gaze toward me. **"I know this woman. I have heard about her through souls passing through. Alanna Sharpe, the Guardsman. You seek the betrayed Sharpe."**

I nod. "Indeed I do. He has been imprisoned within Circle 9 unjustly, and must be released. The fates of many good people rest on my reaching him."

Antaeus seems to consider this. **"I have seen who has imprisoned the betrayed Sharpe, Guardsman. It is one I am familiar with, one who I fought alongside."**

This shouldn't surprise me, but it does. "You know Tyrelius Scolar?"

"I do. We fought great campaigns against Carthage. He was a master tactician. However, our shared past does not excuse his actions now. I will help you."

Antaeus scoops both me and Abaster into his hands, carries us up to his chest, and then lowers us down at his feet, allowing us to set foot on a massive sheet of ice.

Ice ... Dad mentioned ice ... we're close, I know it!

"Good luck, Alanna Sharpe." Antaeus turns his attention back to his duties of guarding the Circle. It takes a minute to gain traction on the slick ice we're now standing on, but I turn to Abaster once I'm confident I won't be slipping and falling anytime soon.

"Welcome to Circle 9," Abaster intones. "This circle of Hell punishes the most insidious sinners of all, traitors. This is also divided into rings. The good news is there are only four of them. The bad news is they are enormous."

I flex my wings, clutching gently at the Sword and my last bottle of holy water. "Bring it. What am I looking at, or looking for?"

Abaster clears his throat slightly. "The first circle we'll encounter is Caina, where traitors to family are frozen. The second is Antenora, where traitors to nations are kept. Third will be Ptolomaea, a place where those who betrayed guests are tormented. The final ring, where the worst sinners are kept, is Judecca, where you will find the souls of those who betrayed lords and benefactors. Also there are the sinners who betrayed God. Our best chances of finding your father will come probably in Caina, Antenora, or Judecca."

I tap my foot on the frozen territory. "Why is there ice here?"

Abaster motions for us to begin walking again, which we do at a slow pace to keep our footing. "Although the entirety of the rest of Hell is superheated, the lowest levels are cold, due to the lack of holiness to be found in these sinners. We currently walk the frozen lake bed of Cocytus, where these sinners are consumed by the ice."

As I'm informed of this, I catch sight of the first round of sinners imprisoned in Caina. Heads stick up from the icy landscape, many of them damaged by frostbite and looking like they have been there for thousands of years. Their faces are frozen slightly downward, and I notice that a number of them weep constantly, their tears freezing into the bases of their necks.

I'm feeling slightly cold myself. I place a hand on the holy water bottle, and realize that it's radiating heat, slightly. I turn to Abaster. "Do you believe my father may be here?"

He nods. "He could be. By taking the side of the Regents, he committed betrayal against his family … yourself, Ariel, and generations of Sharpes that came before him. That would certainly earn him a place among the heads frozen here. We'll simply have to search."

This sounds daunting, especially as there appears to be millions upon millions of heads frozen into this ice. Gingerly stepping around the heads, I start the long and arduous task of searching the faces, trying to find any glimmer of Dad anywhere.

Searching for a righteous needle in a frozen haystack of the damned.

Chapter Twenty-Two: The Admiral

Day 13

I don't think I've been angrier in my entire life. I've wasted two days on a damned wild goose chase.

Abaster and I spent hour on top of hour, looking through the heads sticking out of the ice in Caina. Every single one of them was whimpering, sniveling crybaby, all of them mourning their own fate which they themselves sealed through their sin. Every sob story made me angrier, every excuse built up my stress level.

Eventually, we reached a breaking point when I happened upon another hellbound Sharpe. He looked up at me with a hurt expression, did the usual spiel about wanting to reclaim the Sword for himself, and then told me his story. This was Bertram Sharpe, a Swordbearer who held the role during the War of the Roses and wound up using the Sword against his own children in a fit of insanity.

Since all the Sharpes seem to be attuned to each other, I asked him. "Have you seen my father come through here? Do you know where Cole Sharpe is?"

Bertram sighed and wept. "I wish I could help you, descendant, but I have not seen him, nor have I heard of him being in Caina. I did hear a commotion a while back, but it never stopped. I am sorry."

I sighed and ground my teeth slightly. "Not as sorry as I am."

Abaster finally suggested we camp for the evening, since we had not rested for the entire time we had been in Caina. So now, after wasting a sleepless 34 hours and barely sleeping for three, I'm about ready to snap.

My guide senses this, I think, and tries very gently to lead me forward. "It's time, Alanna, we must move into Antenora."

I grumble and stand up, taking a brief sip off of my last bottle of holy water. I've tried to limit myself to mostly coating the inside of my mouth every time I take a drink, so that it'll last the whole time. I needed two sips yesterday in order to stay awake.

"Antenora is filled with traitors to nations and political benefactors," Abaster recites as we begin walking away from the heads sticking out of the ice. "These were spies and those with treasonous intentions."

While the history would be interesting at another time, I'm more interested in looking for Dad. "Just quit with the lecture and let's search, okay?"

Abaster's mouth twists gently. "All right. Search." He motions around himself. I take that as my cue to start looking for faces.

The problem, however, is that there's a lot of faces that are missing, torn free from the heads they belong to. The sinners here appear to be frozen together in pairs, so they can feed off of each other. Literally, in this case: I watch with disgust as a soul takes a large bite out of another soul's shoulder, leaving a bleeding wound.

The eating soul, though, looks over at me with recognition. "Dear God, why? Why is there a Guardsman here?"

He looks frightened, frozen in the ice. He appears to be mostly naked, but there's one scrap of his clothing remaining, encircling an arm that's out of the ice. It appears to be a uniform sleeve, black with gold striping. I crouch down to face this sinner. "How do you know about the Guardsman?"

He looks down with dismay as he takes a chunk out of the sinner he is frozen over with his teeth. "In life, I guided Guardsmen. I was a handler, sending the Guardsman on his missions."

Something seems familiar about his soul. "What is your name?"

He sighs and clears his throat. "My name is Harris Yardley."

I *do* know this soul. Mom and Dad know him intimately … he was their handler in the CIA. They told me the story of his involvement with their team, and how he sold out to a foreign power and tried to prevent them from rescuing Aunt Kitty when she was captured.

I'm angry at this soul, and I let him know by kicking him. "Damn you then, Yardley. You deserve this punishment." Punctuating my words, the soul he has been devouring turns around and pays him back in kind by taking a bite out of Yardley's throat.

Yardley lets out a gurgling scream. "Let me atone! I know I betrayed the Guardsman, betrayed my country … let me help you! What is your quest?"

I grab Yardley by his hair. "Not that it's your business. I seek my father, Cole Sharpe. He's been brought here unjustly, and I mean to bring his soul back to his body."

Yardley's eyes widen, possibly because he just caught sight of my wings. "Wait … your mother, is Ariel your mother? And Cole is your father …"

I throw down the pathetic soul's head. "What of it?"

He starts to weep. "Please let me atone and help you, daughter of Sharpe and Vibria. It was your parents I betrayed, your parents who revealed my betrayal. Please let me serve my penance to your family!"

I feel anger toward him, anger that I think is justified because of what he did in life. At the same time, though, with his wailing and having large chunks eaten off of him for eternity, I feel some pity for him. I probably shouldn't, but I do finally crouch down and ask for help. "Okay then. You can help me by answering my questions."

"Anything," Yardley stammers.

"Dad was brought down to Hell, into Circle 9. Did you see him at all?"

Yardley's face wrinkles into thought, and then he nods. "There was a group of demons, making loud noises and jeers, who were carrying a struggling soul with them. I remember the soul's voice sounding familiar ... now that you tell me, I think it *was* Cole."

All right, maybe this will be helpful. "Is Dad in Antenora?"

He sighs. "Sadly, no. They rampaged through, but they did not stop."

Damn! "Do you know where they were headed?"

"Not precisely ... although there was one thing the demons mentioned. They were bringing the soul down to *replace* a soul."

This has me confused. "Replace? As in, substitute for another soul?"

Yardley nods. "I think they were switching out Cole for another soul down here."

The light comes on, and my heart gets light. *I know where Dad is!*

"One last thing, Admiral. Were there any significant demons among the group carrying Dad down?"

"Most of them were lower-level devils, nothing to write home about, but one of them ..." Yardley's eyes widen with fear. "Mamuna was with them. She was actually guiding the other little devils, and throwing the most abuse at the soul."

Now I'm thoroughly convinced, Mamuna's involved with the New Empire. Impulsively, I crouch down and gently kiss Yardley's forehead. "Thank you. You've been an immense help to me ... while I can't alleviate your punishment here, please know that at least in my eyes you have paid your penance for your betrayal of Mom and Dad."

Yardley smiles, just as the other soul he's frozen with rips off his bottom lip and consumes it. I stand up and go back over to Abaster.

"Any help to you?"

I nod. "A big help. How long until we get to Judecca?"

Chapter Twenty-Three: Living Hell

Day 17

The journey through Hell has been strenuous. It's been torture on my spirit, on my body, on everything that I believe in. I've felt betrayal. I've felt elation. I've felt anger and sadistic rage, and devastating sorrow. I can only thank God that it's nearly over, and dread what awaits me at the finish line.

Our trek through the remainder of Antenora and all of Ptolomaea took over three days. The rings are too large to fly through without exhausting myself, so we had to walk. I've had the pleasure … so to speak … of observing the punishments of condemned sinners throughout the trail we've taken. I've observed far too much cannibalism for one lifetime, and was very happy to finally leave behind the traitors to nations.

Then we passed through Ptolomaea, with its souls guilty of treason against guests. Even worse than Caina, these sinners only had faces sticking out of the ice. It was also worse because there was no way of walking through without breaking noses with every step.

I can't help thinking that many of the souls weren't dead yet. Dante mentions in the *Inferno* that many of the worst souls are condemned to Hell and reside there even before their bodies die. As I step over familiar looking faces, I can't help but think there might be one or two living souls that I'm stomping on. It makes me uneasy.

We awaken on the cusp of Judecca, greeted by fierce winds and biting cold. I take another sip of holy water … my sipping is getting out of control, as I've drunk a quarter of the final bottle. It does its job, though, and warms me back up. By the time I'm ready to go, Abaster's already waiting for me.

Today it seems like I'm the one who's more eager to continue. "Are you ready?"

He seems a little lifeless today. "I suppose, but ... I need to know, how did you know where your father's going to be after talking to that soul in Antenora?"

I clutch the Sword tightly in my fist. "It was when he mentioned Dad's soul was taking the place of one already here. There's one soul that might think of an idea like that ... the soul of a master tactician, of a man evil enough to betray one of history's most storied rulers for his own gain in another empire. A man evil enough to wield the Sabre of the Invader."

Abaster looks confused. "I don't follow."

"You said it yourself, Judecca is where traitors to lords are punished. We need to find the place where Tyrelius Scolar is *supposed* to be being punished for all of eternity." I place a hand on Abaster's shoulder. "We're going to find Dad today, I'm sure of it. Let's go."

Abaster swallows hard, then steps forward and leads me into the final ring of Circle 9. Immediately, we can feel the air growing ever colder. My own blood chills more, though, when I look up and see a familiar sight, one I saw several days ago: the towering figure of Lucifer, standing at the center of Hell.

Abaster raises his arm toward the despot. *"Vexilla regis prodeunt Inferni."*

This close, I understand why this mega-demon was able to spot me from my mid-air position so far away, as I can see that he has three faces on his head, facing three different directions. Each of the faces chew on souls in their mouths. By the readings of the *Inferno* I'd done to prepare, I remember who those souls were: Brutus and Cassius, who betrayed and assassinated Julius Caesar; and Judas, who betrayed Christ to the Romans.

Suitable punishment for such deep betrayals.

While it's interesting to watch these punishments, I have a job to do. My attention turns to the souls directly close to us, frozen in twisted poses into ice columns. Many of them have shocked expressions on their faces, like they don't understand why they are being punished. There seems to be fewer souls here than in the surrounding rings, though.

"Is it just me, or is it lighter …"

"SWEET JESUS, NO! NOT HER!"

Abaster's panicked cry has me on alert immediately. Clutching the Sword's hilt tighter, I rush over to where my guide is standing. He's bawling, staring into one of the ice pillars.

"What's wrong?"

His wailing is inconsolable. It seems to take all of his effort to point at the soul trapped within the ice, a naked female soul whose face seems familiar …

Then I realize why it's so familiar. It's the Vice President of the New Empire of America. "Is this a living soul? She's still alive and kicking and trying to kill every supernatural on the planet in the living world."

Abaster wails. "Jennifer, why? Why, why have you been sent here? What have you done?" He crumbles before the ice pillar, still weeping. His tears form steamy clouds around his face.

Okay, now I need to know. "How is this soul such trauma for you? What is your knowledge of this woman?"

Abaster looks up and sniffles, tears pouring out of both of his eyes, even more so out of the vacant eye socket. "You don't understand, Alanna. This is my sister. My baby sister, who I took under my wing, who wanted to join my ministry, to help me reach out and save souls … Jennifer, why have you been sent here?" More wailing.

This explains some things. Jennifer Regent apparently started out as Jennifer *Abaster*. The evil she perpetrates in the living world makes her a perfect candidate for living hell, but of all the places she could be, why is she here? What lord did she ... oh wait, she betrayed God. If she was in Abaster's ministry, she's a major betrayer of God.

And it's likely Abaster's going to spend time here, too. I feel compassion for my guide all of a sudden. I crouch down and collect him, try to stand him back up. The urge overcomes me, and I feel the need to embrace this man, to show him some measure of sympathy.

He accepts the hug, lifting his remaining arm to return it. "Thank you, Alanna. I'm sorry, we must continue."

"It's okay. I tell you what, once I'm done here, I'll try my best to save her soul for you, okay?"

Abaster sighs. "I appreciate the gesture, but ... I'm afraid that living souls that come here are beyond saving. The only consolation is that I'll be with my sweet sister once more." His face returns to business. "Come, your father must be nearby."

I look around me, and a familiar face leaps out at me. "Closer than you think." Now it's my turn to start crying, as I step around Abaster and come face to face with a helpless soul being wrongly frozen in an ice pillar.

"Dad ... oh God, Dad, I'm here." My tears start falling, dropping on the base of the ice. He's trapped in a strange position, with both arms pinned over his head and one leg looped behind him. His face looks pained, but his eyes do eventually find mine. His eyes appear to glisten within the ice, even as his lips mouth words at me.

I can't hear him, but he won't stop talking. What's he trying to say? I wish I could read lips better. It looks like ... "turn around?"

When I do, my heart jumps back into my throat. My guide is being run through by the Sabre. Standing behind him is a giant armor-clad man, glaring down at me.

The Invader. The actual Invader.

"Hello, hatchling!" He yanks the Sabre out of Abaster and kicks the damned soul aside. He's standing at least nine

feet tall, brandishing the weapon and waiting for me. I know for sure, especially after hearing the voice, this is Scolar.

"You're the traitor who deserves this punishment, Scolar! What business do you have with Cole Sharpe?"

"Haven't you figured it out yet?" He teasingly sways. *"With your great quest, with your search for your father, haven't you been listening? There's a revolution going on. The New Empire is just the start ... we will soon unleash Hell on Earth, and it will be GLORIOUS!"*

He rushes, Sabre directly in front of him. I barely have time to draw the Sword and meet his thrust, and the sound the two weapons make on contact makes the entire ring shudder. I'm convinced that we've just drawn the attention of every single being within Hell. Scolar continues to slash away, trying to reach me with the weapon.

It's all I can do to block his blows. The Sword feels like it's about to vibrate out of my hands every time it meets his strokes. I need an advantage somehow ... desperate, I take to the air and flutter back away from the swings.

"Come back and fight, coward!" He flings the Sabre at me. Unlike the living world, however, the Invader armor does not disappear: instead, it seems to get larger.

"Who's the true coward? The one who ducks attacks or the one who steals an innocent soul and uses the body?" I tuck my wings and make my own thrust at a weaponless Invader, who slaps me down to the frozen plain. I roll with the blow and return to my feet. Scolar regains his weapon, charges me again ...

I'm dead. Dad, I'm sorry ... wait ...

I catch a fleeting glimpse of Dad's ice pillar. It's starting to crack, originating from the places where my tears struck the ice. An idea strikes me ... an idea that will be catastrophic if it doesn't work.

I put the Sword into one hand and reach behind me, grasping the last bottle of holy water. With my thumb I spin the cap off the bottle.

Scolar sees what I'm doing, and doesn't get it. Instead, he decides to insult me. *"Is this a joke? You plan to defeat me with water? What a pathetic excuse for a warrior ... what are you going to do, splash me to death, HATCHLING?!"*

I take a large swallow of the holy water. I'm going to need all the energy I can manage for this. I cock the arm with the bottle back and fling it, praying that it reaches its target.

Please, God, let this throw work!

The bottle seems to travel in slow motion, holy water splattering out of the opening in a wide arc following the path of the throw. Finally, it strikes its target ... the pillar of ice containing Dad.

The plastic splits on contact. Holy water coats the ice, which immediately starts to crack and melt. The ice finally explodes out from around Dad, releasing his soul as a sputtering heap. Quickly I rush to his side and pull him free of the newly-created hole in Judecca.

I hope I'm right about this ...

Scolar looks at us, crouching down. Then he looks over at where the pillar once was. His eyes go wide. *"No! This can't be! I won't be defeated like this, not by a little girl!"* He screams, dropping his weapon. Dark, hellish energy rises up from the broken pillar, forming tendrils which grasp to every part of Scolar's body, dragging him back to his rightful place among Judecca's condemned. His scream continues unabated until the ice finally rises up to encase him once more.

I stand up and approach the column, Sword still drawn. Scolar's face looks out at me, fearful and panicked. The familiar scars look comical on his surprised expression, as does his pathetic body, twisted into the pose Dad had been frozen into.

My vision goes red. I grit my teeth. *"This little girl just defeated you, once and for all. Enjoy oblivion, you bastard!"*

I bring the Sword back and thrust it cleanly through the ice pillar, and through Scolar's body. I can't hear it, but I watch his face twist into a scream, then collapse into a pocket of dust, permanently sealed into Judecca's icy landscape.

Scolar's gone. Truly dead and gone now.

I can finally sheathe the Sword, so I do. I turn around, away from the pillar. Abaster is just recovering from his injury and starting to stand up, but my attention isn't on him. It's on the soul that remains seated on the frozen ground. I rush to his side and crouch down with him, placing a hand on his shoulder.

"Dad? Dad, please talk to me." My eyes are getting warm again. "Daddy?"

He finally looks up, with a dulled expression on his face. That dullness dissipates, though, as he finally recognizes me. A hand comes up to stroke my cheek. "Alanna ... you did it, you got my message ..."

I'm so happy to see him again ... he's been missing for so long ...

My arms are immediately around Dad, clutching him tightly and weeping into his bare shoulder. He wraps his own arms around me, with all the strength that I remember. We embrace for a long time, our joy untempered by our hellish surroundings.

I've got my Daddy back.

Chapter Twenty-Four: The Damnation Blade

Day 18

Would it be wrong of me to say that it feels good to sleep in Dad's arms? Of course not. To say it feels good to sleep in Dad's arms at the center of Hell? Maybe a little more wrong, I suppose.

Whatever the rightness or wrongness, I'm awakening from the best sleep I've had since Avalon, mainly because my father's soul is free to embrace me and keep me safe. Abaster has helped as well, keeping watch over us all night long.

Dad is awake, too. I suppose the souls don't really have to sleep. "Are you feeling okay, Alanna?"

I nod up at him. "Better than okay, Dad."

He reaches down and pats the Sword gently on my hip. "So Gabe gave it to you, huh? I'm glad. You've been ready to take the birthright for a long time."

There are so many questions I want to ask him … questions about what he's done for Gabe, about how he's managed to survive here … those can wait, though. "Thanks, Dad." I slowly stand up. "Now the trick is how do we get out of here, and how do I contact Pele to open up the gateway back to the living world?"

"Why don't you ask me?" A booming voice that sounds like thunder combined with the erupting of a volcano interrupts the discussion. My blood chills. Everyone's faces look shocked, and I think I know why. We look up above us, and there's the three faces of Lucifer, looking down on us. *"You're looking for the exit, right?"*

Remember what Gabe said ... he's the Lord of Lies ... "I think we know which way to go, actually, thanks." I don't know what to say.

"I was hoping you could help me out, though." He sounds disappointed, for some reason.

"Don't trust him," Abaster is admonishing me. "He's trying to get something out of you that you probably don't want to give."

Dad seems to be concurring with Abaster. "I've had to listen to his crap for what seems like years now. Don't talk to him."

I still have a feeling, though ... there's something more going on here. I look up at the ultimate sinner, up at the three faces which continue to chew on sinners as he talks. "Does this have something to do with Mamuna? I've heard her name come up several times while I've been here."

Lucifer's face darkens ... if that's even possible. *"Indeed. Mammon and his daughter have been planning a coup d'état, and have been creating conditions in the living world that will overload Hell."*

How is that even possible? "How can I trust you?"

"Well, you can't. However, let me fill you in on something you might be interested in." Lucifer lowers one of his massive hands toward the three of us, opening it to reveal an aged leather casket.

"What's this?"

"This is the ultimate weapon. Abaddon, the swordsmith, created two swords. One of them you have already encountered and destroyed."

Okay, he's got that right at least. "Yes, the Sabre has been destroyed. What of it?"

"Let me tell you about it, then, and stop interrupting!" His voice becomes a roar, which shocks me into silence. *"The second weapon, which isn't a cheap copy of an already-existing weapon, was contained in this casket, never to be wielded because it was too powerful. We have come to call it the 'Damnation Blade.'"*

Abaster approaches the casket. "I've seen this around. There is something inside it?"

Lucifer gets a strange look on his face … almost apologetic. *"'Was' is a better word."* The lid of the casket opens, revealing an interior molded to hold a very large sword. Except that there's no sword, it's empty.

Both me and Dad scrutinize the empty space. "This looks like it would've been even bigger than the Sabre. You'd have to be a monster to wield it."

Dad nods in agreement, and then looks up at Lucifer. "Are you saying Mammon stole the weapon?"

"They both did. And they now have it in the living world." Lucifer closes the casket and pulls it away from us. *"Alanna Sharpe, Guardsman, I have an offer to make to you."*

I really don't like the sound of this.

"I want you to find and return this sword to Hell. In return, I will make you a queen among men. You will rule eternally, with your beloved at your side, and no further persecution from those who would see your race extinguished. Refuse me at your peril, though, and watch as your kind die around you."

My hackles are immediately raised. There's so much temptation here. I could ensure everyone I love is safe.

Mom. Dad. Michi. William … but at what cost? I've already lost so much of my humanity in this endeavor. Do I want to give up my soul as well?

My mind is made up. I set my jaw and look up at the Lord of Lies. "I apologize, but my answer is 'no.' I'm afraid I value my soul much higher than you do."

Lucifer seems to shrug. *"Your loss. Don't come crying to me when you're dying."* The massive demon returns to his upright position, resuming his watch over Hell.

So many questions, though … this Blade is more powerful? What can it possibly do above and beyond the Sabre? I'll need some guidance later … I need to remember these things. Right now, though, my priority is escape. I turn to Abaster. "Can you guide us to the exit?"

He sighs and shakes his head sadly. "I must remain here to serve my punishment. The most I can do is point the way. You must go up to Lucifer's body and go straight down." He looks over at Dad. "I'm also afraid that souls have trouble making the trip if they're not attached to bodies. You'll hopefully make it through, but it might be traumatic for you."

I'm afraid now. I don't want to go through all this trouble to lose Dad all over again. I clutch him closer to me. "Hang on tight, Dad, I'll get you out of here." He nods and wraps his arms around my waist. I turn back to Abaster. "Alastair Abaster, you have served me well as my guide. If I can offer you nothing else, please accept my sincere thanks. I'll do my best to save your sister."

Abaster wipes a tear away from his eye. "Good luck and good voyage, Alanna. I wish you nothing but the best." He waves toward us. I turn away from him after waving back, pacing the ice until I find a hole punched through it.

Our escape hatch.

"Hang on, Dad!" I clutch his waist tightly, curl my wings around both of us, and slide down into the hole. Just before we fall through, I spot an inscription carved into the ice next to the opening.

Dante è stato qui, aprile 1300.

I chuckle. *I was here, too.*

I feel the falling sensation shift directions, and realize that I need to open my wings back up, which I do and flap them in the direction I sense to be upward. I look to my side and clutch tighter to Dad, pumping my wings hard and fighting the still air of this place, climbing past the vertically-standing legs of Lucifer, upward more ...

My wings feel like they're going to fall off. Just as I'm about to abandon the effort and give up, though, a familiar voice echoes through the cavern.

"Alanna Sharpe, is that you?"

My heart rises. Dad looks over at me and smiles. I lift my head up. "I'm here, Pele! I'm ready!"

The goddess materializes out of the side of the cavern and flutters her way to us. She grasps both of us and lifts us by our shoulders, zipping past the legs and toward a round opening, through which I can see stars.

Chapter Twenty-Five: Changes

??????????

Ashes are filling my mouth. I'm coated head-to-toe. I don't know where I've emerged, but it's someplace almost as filthy as where I came from. I shake some of the ashes off of my hair and face, and pull myself out of the hole I'm coming out of.

The first sensation I have is that I'm damned tired. Eighteen days' worth of fatigue is catching up to me in eighteen seconds. I have barely enough strength to get out of the hole and collapse on my knees.

The second sensation is panic. I'm alone. *Pele! DAD!* Neither of them came out of the hole with me. My heart is racing. On instinct, I reach for the Sword ...

... and a sensation of utter peace overcomes me. There's a reassuring presence I can feel when I hold the hilt of my family's weapon. *He's with me. We're almost home, Daddy.*

My reverie is interrupted by searchlights and loud sirens. The last thing I want is a fight, but it looks like one's coming to me. I hear someone with a bullhorn over the mess. *"Alanna Sharpe, stay where you are! You are in the custody of the Supernatural Suppression Agency!"*

Well, I know I'm back in the living world. Worse, though, I've emerged vulnerable in the New Empire, with barely any energy and nobody to help me. I raise my hands above my head. "I surrender! Don't shoot!"

Apparently, they don't want to take me prisoner, as I hear several weapons being cocked and readied to fire. The bullhorn voice appears again. *"Weapons at the ready, shoot to kill on my mark!"*

I swallow hard. I'm not going to buy it from an impromptu firing squad. My hand is making its way for the Sword ...

"CONCUSSION!"

A familiar female voice booms through the night, and I watch as every searchlight on me is blasted away in one single blow. It's at this point that my entire lack of energy catches up to me, and I fall over on my side. I'm only vaguely aware of people rushing to my side, voicing concern. I only hear half-snippets of words.

"... glad Gabe knew where to be ..."

"... been gone so long, I wasn't sure she'd be coming back ..."

"... hurry it up and get her out of here ..."

The bustle isn't enough to keep me conscious, as I slip into a deep sleep.

??????????

I awaken, groggy but aware that I've been put into a bed. It's soft. It's familiar-feeling. I open up my eyes and spot another familiar sight, a snarling mountain lion head standing guard over me. I'm immediately at ease. The blankets feel much better than I'm used to.

I finally have the energy to lift up my head, and look around the room. Am I alone? Not quite, there's a large figure standing by the door. He walks into the light, slowly but with friendly intent.

"You're awake ... thank the Creator."

I smile, and tears fall. "William ..." My voice is a hoarse creak. "... William, oh God I'm so happy to be home ..."

He chuckles. "I'm glad, too. I've missed you so much." My eyes find the familiar face, smiling, but different. He looks ... older? He has scars across his forehead now, and a long one along his cheek.

They've been fighting ... oh God, they've been fighting too hard without me ...

He sits down on the edge of the bed next to me. I sit up and his arms are immediately around me, clutching me as desperately as I clutch him. His body feels amazing against mine ... I've missed his warmth, his embrace, his wondrous presence ...

"How long have I been gone, William?"

He shudders. "How long has it been for you?"

I know this is going to make me sad, but I answer him anyway. He has a right to know, after all. "Eighteen days. It took me that long to get through the place."

He sighs deeply. "Well then ... in that case, I've got good news and bad news for you." He reaches behind him and produces a cupcake with a single candle sticking out of it. "On the good side, happy birthday."

I can't help but giggle ... it's too cute. I take the cupcake from him and look into his eyes. "What's the bad news?"

He clears his throat. "You just turned nineteen today."

July 4th, 2031

Two years, gone. The shock is still settling into me as I get dressed. After dropping the bomb on me, William invited me to breakfast with the others. It's going to be rough this morning, even now that I know this. How much fighting has been seen over the last two years? What ... who ... is going to be waiting for me at the table? Aunt Kitty, Uncle Cyrus, Michi, Fahaian ... William didn't tell me anything about the others, just came to wish me happy birthday, hug me, then left.

The closet is filled with unfamiliar clothing. None of the outfits I kept here are present, probably in storage because they didn't know when I would be coming back. I resign myself to a basic t-shirt and jeans combo, wincing as I put on the shirt and my shoulder disagrees with the motion. The pants aren't much easier to do, either. I must have seriously hurt myself down there ... maybe I can have Grandmother check it out.

If Grandmother is still around.

My attention turns to the clothes I wore through Hell. Obviously ruined, they look like they've been soaking for a year in a septic tank, and smell about the same. It's depressing for me, though, because it's Mom's uniform that I ruined trying to get to Dad. Even through the crud caked on it, the embroidered lettering that spells out VIBRIA can still be seen.

My eyes feel warm again, but not out of sadness. My mind shifts toward duty. *It's Mom's turn to be saved now.*

That is, if I even saved Dad.

I turn and look at myself in the mirror just before stepping out of the room. Still me, the same teenage girl I was. Maybe I'm a little on the scuffed side ... I've got some cuts on my face and a few bruises from my journey ... but I'm still me. I'm technically an adult now, but I'm still me. Right?

I look just over my shoulders, and notice that for the first time in a long time, my wings are retracted. I was almost afraid that I'd never be able to pull them back again, that I'd have to keep them out for the rest of my life. They feel dully painful, but none the worse for the wear and tear of the Inferno. Satisfied that I'm still myself, I steel myself for what I'll be heading toward at the breakfast table.

One last thing. The Sword resumes its place at my hip. If at all possible, I'm never taking it off again.

The hallway seems so much longer than I remember. Maybe because I'm dreading the other end? How much change is there going to be? How much have my friends changed? The world? Me? Sooner than I would have liked, the light of day greets me ...

... and a bright orange streak leaps across the room and glomps me. "ALANNA!"

I know the voice for sure, it's just the body that's confusing. When I see what's hugging me, it's a girl who looks like she's more tiger than human. There's some things that are still familiar, one of those being the long leather glove coating her entire left arm.

I'm tentative, but I finally manage to say it. "Michi?"

She grins, and I see her teeth are sharpened to points to go along with the cat body. "You got it! I missed you so much!" She literally picks me up and leaps over to the table again.

"Michika Salem, you put her down right now! The last thing she needs is you snapping her spine because you don't know your own strength!"

Aunt Kitty's voice sounds strained, not near the jovialness I was used to before. I get put down into a seat, and then Michi's cat face takes on an exaggerated expression of regret. "Sorry, Mom. I'm still getting used to this."

Aunt Kitty simply sighs. "I know. God, I know." She rolls her eyes, sipping on a cup of tea. "Alanna, we're happy to have you back among the living. It's been too long."

She supportively puts her hand on mine and squeezes. I appreciate the gesture, but ... something's not right. "Where is everyone?"

Michi slides a plate of Aunt Kitty's cooking in front of me. *Sweet Jesus, I haven't eaten in so long ...* I take up a fork and voraciously rip into the bison steak and fried eggs in front of me. Michi sits down next to me.

"It's complicated, actually. Fahaian's back in Jordan, unfortunately his dad died so he had to take the throne."

I swallow hard, I'm sure for the first of many times. "So he's *King* Fahaian now?"

Michi nods kind of sadly. It's clear she misses him. "So yeah, he's in Jordan. The numbers of supernaturals going through the Avalon door have started to dwindle, mainly because the New Empire's doubling down on supernaturals. It's getting tougher for us, to be honest." She sighs deeply. "For the most part, the folks from the refuge have all passed through, and those of us who are still here at the Ranch are the ones who are able-bodied to defend it."

I turn to Aunt Kitty. "Who all is here?"

"Well, the two of us, and William obviously. Trent Gracin and Teresa Iles have been acting as support for us, as has Jerry Tile. Cyrus is coordinating all the supernaturals in Avalon, and he took Julian with him."

"What about Grandmother? And Gabe?"

A knock on the door stops Aunt Kitty from answering. She stands up and opens it, allowing two figures to enter. One of them lights up when she spots me.

"Alanna! We're so happy you're back again!" Grandmother rushes over to my side and embraces me. "Are you hurt?"

"I'm okay, but I might ask you to take a look at some things later," I reply with a smile. My happiness fades, however, when the second figure comes over to the table, sipping on a bottomless cup of coffee.

"Alanna, it's heartening that you've made it back."

I stand up and face toward Gabe across the table. "Not that you care, Gabe, but I managed to get through it well enough. What was the point of all of that? Making me lose two years, putting me literally through Hell? Was it really worth it?"

He smirks. "You tell me. As for the point, you need to realize that victory without righteousness will be no better than stumbling through Hell again. You can't win this war if you lose your soul at the same time."

I'm about to explode at this new riddle, but then I realize that he's right. I *had* to see the torments of Hell, to fully understand the stakes we fight for here on Earth. We have to prevent that from being unleashed upon innocents.

My hand drifts down to the Sword. "I need to see Dad."

All of us immediately rush down the hallway, to the room where Dad has been laid out. William is the one who greets us when the door opens, but I'm the only one who enters the room.

"How is he?"

William shakes his head. "Still like he's been, for two years. Still just that blank stare, but the muttering stopped a while back."

I think I know why. I slowly make my way over to the bed, unstrapping the Sword from around my waist. I kneel next to the prone figure of my father, not knowing whether I'm taking the right action, hoping I've done this correctly. My eyes close in prayer.

Lord God, please let this man come back. Let me have my father back.

I lay the Sword along Dad's body, with the hilt on his chest. I place the hand closest to me over the engraving of the Sharpe name on the finger guard. My own hands remain over his.

"Please, Daddy, come back to us."

I press the Sword tighter into Dad's chest. *It feels unusually warm ...*

There's a loud gasp, which makes me jump backward. The Sword flies off of Dad's body and back into my hands. I look up at his face, to his eyes. They are wide open, and no longer blankly staring. He blinks. He turns his head to look at me.

He smiles. *Daddy's smiling at me!*

"Alanna ..."

I race over to his side and clutch him tightly to me. "Daddy ... welcome home."

To Be Concluded ...

More to Come ...

The journey through Hell is over, and Alanna's father is back to himself. The war in the living world, however, has raged on for two years in her absence, as the New Empire has signed a death warrant on supernaturals worldwide.

The changes that have taken place will take her by surprise. New powers wielded by her best friend, dwindling numbers of allies, and a new resolve by Jennifer Regent to destroy Alanna will complicate her new purpose: rescuing her mother from the New Empire's clutches.

Her attempts to reunite with Ariel will culminate in a final, decisive battle, as a woefully outnumbered supernatural force faces the entire Supernatural Suppression Agency ... led by their new demonic commander and a terrifying weapon, the Damnation Blade.

If Alanna and her party falls ... supernaturals in every plane of existence will perish.

EDEN
INVIOLATE
**The *final* chapter of the
Phantom Squadron saga
Coming Soon from
Desert Coyote
Productions**